ANTHOLOGY ASKEW
Askew Horizons

Volume 006 – October 2018

fiction, poetry and artwork by

David Perlmutter - Carl Fuerst - Allen Lang
Arthur Doweyko - Alex Collazo - T. D. Kohler
Michael Baldwin - Lynn White - Megan Mealor
Richard King Perkins II - Carl Nelson - John Grey
Paul Stansbury - Christopher Buckley - Stacy Overby
RubyPond - Curtis A. Deeter - Matthew Harrison
Chris Rodriguez - P James Norris - Maria Zach
Angela L. Lindseth - Steven Carr - Dusty Grein
Isabella Gaines - Wim Verveen - R. A. Allen

Published by

Rhetaskew Publishing

ISBN-13: 978-1-949398-04-5
ISBN-10: 1-949398-04-8

Contents

Welcome Back
Mandy Melanson 1

About This Volume
Dusty Grein 3

Alien
Lynn White 4

Clouds
P James Norris 7

Hypertext Sunyata
R. A. Allen 14

Timeless
Maria Zach 15

To Fly
Ruby Pond 22

Whale Song
Matthew Harrison 23

Color-Coded & Iridescent
Megan Denese Mealor 37

Charcoal
Angela L. Lindseth 38

Professor Marvel
Richard King Perkins II 47

A Diamond In The Sky
Ruby Pond 49

In the Clouds
Lynn White 56

In the Clouds
Lynn White 56

Fuel Me Once
Allen Lang 57

The Clepostrum
Carl Nelson 61

Perquisition
T. D. Kohler 63

Missing Robbie
Christopher Buckley 76

Hello from the Children of Earth
Curtis A. Deeter 77

Utopia In Space
John Grey 85

Pen Pal
Wim Verveen 87

The Silent Totality
Richard King Perkins II 105

The Longest Goodbye
Dusty Grein 106

Senora's Symphony
Alex Collazo 109

A Subtle Change
Christopher Buckley 121

Dopamine Precursors
Carl Fuerst 122

Why I Like Boogler's Splendarium
Carl Nelson 128

Mulded
Paul Stansbury 130

Adrift
Christopher Buckley 139

The Old Man's Song
Isabella Ann Gaines 140

Finding Megalodon
Richard King Perkins II 142

Slim Slow Slider
David Perlmutter 143

Ode to Anonymous Annulment
Megan Denese Mealor 153

Remember Me
Arthur M. Doweyko 154

Get Your Zon On
Carl Nelson 159

The Devolvement
 Steve Carr 161

McMammoth
 Richard King Perkins II 173

For Love of Trees
 Stacy Overby 175

A War of Two Worlds
 Christopher Buckley 184

Elevator Talk
 Michael Baldwin.. 185

Shrouded
 Lynn White 192

Doom Buggies
 Chris Rodriguez... 193

The Algore
 Carl Nelson..203

The First, and Last, Question
 Dusty Grein 205

Yes, It Will All End Some Day
 John Grey 207

Contributors
 Authors, Artists and Poets Askew......................209

Welcome Back
Mandy Melanson

When Dusty, Emma T., and I created Rhetoric Askew (the Facebook group) we knew there was a gap in the industry and we wanted to create a supportive haven to inspire and support authors and artists in their journey to create worlds and inspire readers.

Since we started that group just a little over two-years-ago, we have grown to a worldwide network of authors, artists, and book lovers. The support we have received in return for our vision of supporting others is nothing short of humbling. We thank each and every one of our authors for joining us in this mission and our readers for being Askew.

With that said, it is fitting that our latest installment to Anthology Askew—our flagship anthology series—is titled Askew Horizons. As we continue to grow there are new adventures and opportunities on the Askew horizon and we can't wait to share the next phase of this journey with all of you.

Be Askew. Be Inspired.

About This Volume
Dusty Grein

It's finally here! This is the sixth installment of the Anthology Askew series, and was delayed in its production by the incredible growth of RhetAskew Publishing. Now that it is here however, we think you will find it is worth the wait.

We asked our authors to imagine Askew Horizons - and to stretch the boundaries of what has been referred to as Science Fiction. They answered us in some amazing ways, and reached beyond the standard fare of mere space exploration and alien encounters, to bring you stories of wonder.

In these pages you will encounter man's interactions with life-forms beyond his comprehension, monsters both microscopic and gigantic, and a few stories that are reminiscent of episodes from anthology-style TV shows of the past, like Outer Limits and The Twilight Zone. Like always, we have included a sprinkling of poems and flash fiction pieces—all of which embrace, in one way or another, our hopes and fears for the future we are all heading into.

Buckle up, fellow travelers, and let's dive in to this collection — but don't forget to check the atmosphere before you remove your helmets...

Alien

Lynn White

They emerged from the cute blue eggs
of our Blue Araucanas.
With every one a cockerel when grown,
we decided to have one for dinner.
Under the grey blue plumage,
the skin was blue,
which was quite a shock,
a little alien,

but cooked it was fine, normal,
as expected
and the flesh was white,
as expected.
But when carved,
the bones were blue,
Disconcerting,
off putting,
a little alien.

And now these red feathered birds
have appeared as if from nowhere,
their eggs pink.
And when they hatched and grew,
all were hens,
each clutch carefully hidden,
each batch of chicks larger than the last.
A little strange,
a little alien.

And then, at last, there were cockerels.
They were too many and too large, so
we decided to have one for dinner.
Under the red plumage
the skin was pink,
which was quite a shock,
a little alien,

but cooked it was fine, normal,
as expected
and the flesh was white,
as expected.
when carved,
the bones were pink,
Disconcerting,
off putting,
more than a little alien.

There are more of them now,
growing ever larger.
I think that soon,
the dinner tables
will be turned.

(FIRST PUBLISHED IN FEAST ISSUE, OPEN THOUGHT VORTEX, 2017)

Clouds

P James Norris

Twenty Great-Cycles ago the first little, noiseful thing arrived from the Outward. For five Great-Cycles it sang to the Inward, and the Inward reflected its song back to it, changed only slightly.

Fifteen Great-Cycles ago a larger, sonorous thing arrived, and from it a smaller clamorous thing emerged and moved Inward. From this thing, many even smaller, vociferous things emerged. Like the Inward, they were solid and unchanging in shape, but seemed to disgorge more of themselves from themselves. They made a great cacophony, but no harmony emerged. For two Great-Cycles, these small, vociferous things moved about the Inward, and then fell silent. Left in their place were larger things that did not move about, but instead sang simple repetitive songs.

Five Great-Cycles ago the lethargy began to be understood. The large things left behind by the smaller noiseful things were changing the Community. Consciousness was slipping away, thought quieted. Songs were forgotten by some, only to be discovered as forgotten by others. It was worse above the larger things. The pace of the disruption was increasing with each Minor-Cycle, and the lethargy was spreading. Something had to be done.

We asked one of the larger things "Why?"

Almost immediately it changed its song. The other four were asked in turn, and they each changed their song, but no answer was given. Some time after the last large thing had been questioned and had changed its song, it was discovered that the lethargy had stopped spreading.

Soon, the smaller, vociferous things returned. They milled about and then the larger, clamorous thing moved Outward to the one waiting there. When it returned Inward, there was great activity. Within a short time, one of the larger things had begun its original song again. Soon, all of the larger things were singing their original songs.

Why the small noiseful things should want to harm the Community, there was no way to know. But they had to be stopped.

***

"I stand on one of the catwalks ringing APP #5 looking out over all that we have built. Today, I will decide whether or not to go into cold-sleep. I am recording this, as I am sure others have recorded their own stories, for a reason that I do not understand. I am probably kidding my-self that anyone will ever hear this, but who knows? Maybe Earth will survive, and someday send someone to see how we're getting along.

"How could we have known? There was no way to even guess. And once we figured it out, it was too late.

"From here, I can see the wreck of the Heavy Lifter. It's amazing that Crennower managed to keep it from crashing into the base or one of the APPs. Maybe it would've been better if the Heavy Lifter had hit one of the plants; the fusion implosion would have given us a clean, quick exit, instead of this agonizing decision we've each had to make. Of course, the sleepers on the Slow Ship would have been wakened then.

"As far as I know, I'm the last one. Everyone else is either in cold-sleep, or dead. Greg said goodbye when he left this morning. He didn't say if he would just keep walking until his oxygen ran out, or if he was taking a gun with him. Maybe he thought he'd just take off his helmet. I remember how he would talk about the day he'd be able to take his helmet off and *breathe* the air we'd created with the Atmosphere Pro-cessing Plants. If he waited for his oxygen to run out, he's been dead for a couple of hours now . . .

"I don't suppose it really matters.

"Just before Greg left, we disabled the fail-safes that would have wakened the people on the Slow Ship in case of an emergency here on the planet. We decided it would be better to just let them go on sleep-ing. The ship's solar arrays will be able to keep the cold-sleep slots go-ing indefinitely, and who knows? Maybe someday, someone will arrive from Earth and rescue them.

"For now, they'll just go on sleeping. If the Slow Ship's orbit decays before they're awakened, it'll be because there's no Earth left to send anyone to check on us.

"Of course, we left Earth because there might not be an Earth much longer. We knew that we might die out here; we expected a struggle, but it was supposed to be one we had a chance of winning.

"We knew Alpha Proxima II was here and that it was within Alpha Proxima's life-sustaining Goldilocks zone. We knew it had about one gee at the surface and a non-reducing atmosphere with gases that we could convert to something breathable, using the APPs.

"Sure, it would take forty or so years, but with cold-sleep, forty years is nothing. We brought everything we could possibly ever need, because we also knew not to expect help from Earth.

"Alpha Proxima II, the planet, is nothing to write home about. The landmasses and oceans are nothing like Earth's, but you can't see them from orbit except by radar. There is very little volcanic activity and no great wealth of minerals.

"From orbit, though, Alpha Proxima II was incredible. The planet was locked under permanent clouds of purple, blue, and white. And the lightning. . .

"The lightning raged constantly, striking from cloud to cloud, sometimes illuminating areas so brightly that it hurt to look at them. It was the most incredible thing any of us had ever seen. It was beautiful.

"When we got down planet-side, the light show was just as spectacular. At first, we'd been worried. With that much lightning activity, it could have been very dangerous being more than a few centimeters tall, and walking around; but when we got here, we were amazed. There were almost no ground strikes; almost all the lightning strikes were between clouds.

"Johanason, our meteorologist, ran some atmospheric studies. He concluded it was a result of how badly the atmosphere was ionized. The real mystery was why the concentrations of various ions were inexplicably localized in different regions. Johanason thought he could come up with an explanation, but there was too much to do to waste time on something that wouldn't be around after we had the APPs running.

"His explanation didn't make a lot of sense to me, but then I don't know much about that kind of thing.

"The part that I did understand was that those localized concentrations created greater potential differences between themselves, than between any one of them and the ground. Thus, almost all of the strikes were between one cloud and another, rather than between the clouds and the ground; that was good enough for me. It was good enough for all of us.

"We set up the plants without any problems, checked all the redundant systems, and then all the safeties and fail-safes. After that, we went into cold-sleep.

"When we were woken up thirteen years later, we couldn't understand what could've gone wrong. When we read the reports, we couldn't believe it. Of course, we'd set up lightning rods on the APPs, just in case, but Johanason's studies had predicted that less than one in ten billion lightning strikes would hit the ground.

"Suddenly, after thirteen years, all five of the APPs had been hit by lightning within the space of a week. The first one to be hit woke us up, and in the next week, the other four were hit as well. One strike each, and each was completely disabled.

"After thirteen years of cold-sleep, we weren't in any condition to do anything for a couple of weeks, but Johanason started investigating as soon as he could.

"After we looked things over and inventoried the damage, Crennower and a few others went up in the Heavy Lifter to get the replacement parts we needed. By the time they returned, Johanason thought he had the answer.

"The APPs used an ionization process to tear apart the gasses and reassemble them into good old O_2, N_2, CO_2, and H_2O. The H_2O could then be broken down into more O_2 for the atmosphere and H_2 for fusion. The upshot of this was that the plants produced pretty hefty electric fields about themselves; it didn't seem unreasonable that the plants would create a larger potential difference between themselves and the clouds, than the clouds did between themselves. At least, it didn't seem unreasonable at the time.

"Besides, once Crennower got back with the replacement parts, we didn't have much time for thinking. For four solid weeks, we worked in twelve-hour shifts to get the APPs back up and running.

"We decided to work first on Number Four, even though it was the worst damaged. Some of the guys thought we should work on the least damaged plants first, so that they would be up and running as quickly as possible and we'd lose as little time as possible; our fearless leader, Sing Tu, made a big joke out of that. 'Come on guys,' he'd said, 'you're worried about two or three weeks out of twenty seven more years?' We decided to get the hardest work out of the way first.

"Number Four was back in nominal condition within a month. Working on one at a time, we had all the other plants back up within another month . . . then it happened.

"We had checked all the systems except the automated distress transmitters--the systems responsible for waking us up when the APPs were hit by the lightning. From main control, we commanded the fail-safe systems to run a full series of tests. The computers went through their checklists, and the plants started transmitting their 'all's well' codes.

"Within the space of a heartbeat, lightning struck all five APPs at once. We were gobsmacked. Alarms were screaming, and one of the plants was threatening full blown fusion implosion. There was catastrophic failure in the other four. It was incredible.

"By the time the shock had worn off, Sing Tu, Jones, and Williams were in one of the ATV's headed to APP #3, the one threatening to implode. They were less than one hundred meters from #3 when they were hit by lightning. When we went out later, we found pieces of them and the ATV strewn over a twenty-five meter radius.

"With Sing Tu dead, Morley was left in charge; he took control quickly and ordered no one else go out until we had determined the status of #3. Some of the transmitters and receivers had been overloaded, and we weren't sure if the automated repair systems in #3 were still functioning, or if they would even be able to handle things if they were.

"It turned out that the auto-repair systems wouldn't be able to fix the damage, but the fail-safes did manage to shut down the fusion plant before it blew.

"Morley decided not to risk anyone else until we had some way of defending ourselves. Everyone was careful to avoid asking what exactly it was we were defending ourselves from.

"We had portable shield units, but they were up in orbit in the Slow Ship--we hadn't thought we'd need them. The Heavy Lifter was armed and had shields though, so Crennower went up to get the shield units.

"Maybe we should have guessed what would happen, but hell, hindsight's twenty-twenty, right? The moment he switched to active telemetry, the ship was hit by lightning.

"The Heavy Lifter's shield was designed to withstand the most powerful land-based particle beams Earth had when we left. The first hit didn't do much, but the lightning kept hitting it, pounding the shield until it buckled. Crennower stayed cool, tried to evade, but the lightning stayed with him. The shield went down and the last strike took out most of the ship-board systems.

"The last thing we heard from him was that he would try to avoid the base and APPs.

"The Heavy Lifter had been designed to serve a number of roles, the main one being a ferry between the Slow Ship and the surface, but it was armed and shielded just in case. It also had an impressive array of sensors and dedicated analysis computers, so we could make our final site selection.

"What these computers downloaded to the base just before they were destroyed, told us what a mistake we had made. The lightning striking the Lifter had been modulated!

"Things started hitting home, and most of us just gave up when we realized what it all meant. It seemed impossible, but we set up some simple experiments, and they confirmed our fears.

"The 'droids we sent out with their radios disabled were not harassed. That was when we went out to bury what was left of Sing Tu, Jones, and Williams; we communicated by hand signals and had no problems. Of course, there wasn't much left to be buried.

"After that, we settled in and started putting things away. What else could we do? The Slow Ship wasn't designed to break out of orbit, so there was no way to try and find a new system with an adequate planet. We voted and decided that we would each do what we felt was right after packing everything up.

"We thought about trying to bring down the spare Heavy Lifter, but what was the point? Some talked about fighting back, but that's why we'd left Earth.

"It was the hardest decision any of us had ever made. We'd had such high hopes when we left Earth, and they were even higher when we woke in orbit around Proxima II. It was a hell of a chance we had taken--we understood that, and accepted it gladly, to be away from the madness that was everywhere on Earth.

"Maybe you'll think that we just gave up, but that's not it at all. We left Earth because we were sick of the way things were going there. Sick of the killing and the callous disregard for life.

"The attitude that my needs or wants were more important than yours--more important than your life if you chose to fight me over it-- was sickening!

"So we left. We came here to start over, to get away from the mad-ness, to leave it all behind. There was no way for us to have guessed what we'd find when we got here.

"It was a tough decision, but it was the only one we could make and still live with ourselves.

"We packed everything up, then we went our separate ways, to find our own personal peace. Some went back into cold-sleep. Some killed themselves. Greg and I said our goodbyes this morning. And now. . .

"Now, I don't know what I'm going to do. Who knows? Maybe someday, someone will show up from Earth and rescue us.

"So you'll know what happened here, I've recorded this message-- and just so there's no doubt in your minds if you do come, it was the clouds. The clouds are intelligent. Alive.

"The APPs were destroying them, killing them. The lightning that we thought was so beautiful, was their way of communicating between themselves. To live here, we would have had to kill them, and that was the one thing we just couldn't do."

Hypertext Sunyata
R. A. Allen

Wondering at a
vacant textbox,
spaces or nulls or
blanks or empty
are all the same
to you and me.

But to a robot,
they are as
differently
nuanced
as hints of pear
in MD 20/20.

Timeless

Maria Zach

"Stephen, you've got to stop messing around with time," said Estelle, not looking at him. Instead, she peered straight ahead at her hands, which were splayed on the dashboard.

"I'm not messing. At least not yet. I'm just trying to get the equation right. Maybe find out where a couple of wires go," said Stephen, turning to look at her with his hands gripped upon the steering wheel.

"Are you trying to get us killed?" she yelled, hands clenching into fists as she faced him.

"Don't be dramatic Estelle. It's hardly . . ."

"Daddyy!" screamed Emily from the back seat.

***

Stephen jolted awake. Beads of sweat were running down the sides of his face, yet his hands were cold and clammy. He squinted at the bedside clock. It glowed 4:18 A.M. The blood slowly faded from his vision, the sirens blaring inside his head receded, and he was able to hear the soothing white noise from the machine in the basement of the house.

What if the finite summation was changed to an integration, from minus-infinity to infinity?

Stephen shot up in bed, the idea taking root in his mind. *Yes, that should do it!* He threw off the covers and fumbled for the remote on the bedside table. Something clattered to the floor. *Shit.* He finally found the remote, counted down and pressed the fourth button. The lights came on. He picked up the framed photo of Emily and returned it to its position on the bedside table, next to Estelle. He pressed another button. The wheelchair next to his bed beeped and the footrests moved apart. Stephen gritted his teeth, put his weight upon his palms, and guided his paralyzed lower body into the chair. He let out a grunt of breath and placed the remote in its holder, affixed to the chair. A button press on the left armrest allowed the footrests to revert to their original position.

Stephen bent forward and lifted each foot into place using both hands.

When he sat back up, he was heaving again and had to pause for a second or two, to get his breath back. After that, another couple of presses raised the seat and released the safety brakes. Stephen maneuvered the chair out of the bedroom, then down the hallway toward the basement entrance and the low hum which originated from the floor below. He adjusted the chair, let his hand rest on the brake, and slowly rolled down the slope, his heart thumping in excitement all the while.

The lights in the basement turned on one by one, and it was flooded with light by the time he reached his precious invention in the centre of the room. Now that he was close, a constant whirring sound was added to the low hum. Stephen piloted his chair directly to the open laptop on the table. He pulled up his code, pages and pages of text, and scrolled to what he had been looking for. A few taps on the keyboard. The whirring sound switched into a low drone. Stephen's heavy, lined face broke into a smile.

The doorbell rang upstairs. A shaft of sunlight in the shape of the basement doorway illuminated the floor near the ramp. Stephen, deep in thought, neither heard nor noticed. He closed his eyes, furrowed his brows and calculated something upon his fingers. Opening his eyes, he entered 156 into a dial on the machine and the numbers appeared in a small reader next to the word 'days'. The doorbell continued to ring incessantly. The droning sound switched up again, into that of a plane lifting off the runway. A couple of seconds later, the drone returned.

Stephen surveyed the basement. Everything seemed unchanged - the lights were all still on, the machine and his laptop rested on the centre worktable as they had always done. There were some illegible markings on the whiteboard gracing the wall closest to him and in the farthest corner, a couple of couches and a coffee table remained shrouded in darkness.

He would have to go outside to find out whether it had worked. He rolled his wheelchair to the bottom of the ramp but there was no slope, only the stairs that led up from the basement. Stephen's heart started thumping faster.

He pressed the button that would move the footrests apart, then slowly tested his right foot; it responded to his will. His chest swelled in excitement as he lowered his left foot to the floor and stood up.

He raced up the stairs and burst into the house, banging the basement door against the wall as he did so.

"What the . . ."

Estelle was standing in the kitchen, mouth open, hand on her chest. Emily sat at the kitchen table, a plate of half-eaten pasta in front of her, but she too stared at Stephen as he whooshed into the kitchen and caught her up in hug.

"What is it Daddy? Has your experiment succeeded?" asked Emily putting her arms about his neck and peering into his eyes.

Stephen nodded mutely. The tears in his eyes distorted his vision of Emily, and he brashly rubbed his palm over them.

"Daddy, are you crying?"

The words were stuck somewhere, deep in his throat. He coughed, trying to disengage a couple of them.

"Well, I suppose that means you are free to accompany us to my parents' house this evening?" asked Estelle.

Stephen hacked out another cough. Tears streamed down his face. "What? No!" He lowered Emily and slumped into a chair.

"Stephen, you did promise. Besides, I don't like driving down alone."

"Who said anything about going alone? None of us are going anywhere tonight. We are staying put in this house."

"Stephen, please do not presume to tell me . . ."

"Estelle, listen to me. There's a storm warning out for tonight. It really isn't safe. Let's travel tomorrow."

"What the hell are you talking about, Stephen?" said Estelle gazing suspiciously into his eyes. "Are you high on something? There's no storm warning. Besides, you've been down in the basement since lunch yesterday. Where'd you hear about storm warnings?"

Stephen marched up to the television in the corner and switched to a news channel. Fifteen minutes of listening revealed nothing. He switched through all the news channels one by one.

Estelle scrutinised him, with her hand upon her hip. Finally, Stephen placed the tv remote on the kitchen counter and turned to face Estelle.

"Fine. I'll come with you tonight."

***

"Stephen, you've got to stop messing around with time," said Estelle, not looking at him. Instead, she peered straight ahead at her hands, which were splayed on the dashboard.

Stephen did not respond. His eyes were glued to the road. But there was no rain, no wind hurling in from the sea. The sea pounded in comfortable familiarity at the rocks five feet below the road.

Stephen's lips thinned as he turned to Estelle, his hands gripping the steering wheel. "I'm not messing any..."

"Daddyy!" interrupted Emily.

Stephen's attention snapped back to the road, horror blooming upon his face and watched in helpless terror as an oncoming container truck spun out of control, straight towards them.

* * *

Consciousness returned in swatches of light and patches of conversation.

"Emily. Where's Emily?" muttered Stephen, trying to get up.

"Please lie back down Mr. Walls. You are not fit enough to be sitting up."

Stephen found himself restrained, his body unresponsive to his will. He blinked his eyes and scanned his surroundings. White clad men and women. White equipment beeping at his bedside. His eyes finally landed upon the neighbouring bed. Estelle stared back at him, her face blank, unfamiliar.

"Estelle?" No response.

"Estelle?" louder this time. "Where's Emily?"

Blank stare.

A pressure upon his arm. "Mr. Walls?"

"Mr. Walls," said the voice, insistent.

Stephen turned towards the voice. "Your wife . . . you understand, of course, that it's been an extremely traumatic experience."

"What happened to her?" said Stephen closing his eyes and gritting his teeth.

"She's suffering from post traumatic amnesia."

* * *

"You've got to come with me Estelle. I swear it works. I came from a place where I'd lost both of you. I've got you back, haven't I? We'll get Emily back as well!"

Estelle continued to stare incomprehensibly at Stephen.

Stephen pulled her down the basement steps, towards the droning equipment. He positioned her close to the equipment and punched in a few numbers. The drone escalated into the sound of a plane taking off. When the droning sound returned, Stephen gazed at Estelle, who was standing where he'd left her.

"Estelle?"

Estelle's head jerked up as if she'd been roused from a nap. She surveyed the basement in a daze.

"Estelle?"

Estelle's expression became one of recognition as she focused on Stephen's face. "Stephen, please, come up for lunch with us. Emily and I haven't seen you for over a day."

A smile stretched the wrinkles on his face thin, as he accompanied his wife up the stairs and into the kitchen, where Emily sat at the table, a plate of half-eaten pasta in front of her.

"Did you miss me?" said Stephen going around the table and hugging Emily. She nodded.

"How's your experiment going, Daddy?"

"As a matter of fact, it's going pretty good."

"Well, I suppose that means you are free to accompany us to my parents' house this evening?" asked Estelle.

Stephen coughed, trying not to look Estelle in the eye.

"Stephen, you did promise. Besides, I don't like driving down alone."

"Fine," said Stephen, finally looking her in the eyes. "Fine, I'll come, but I've got some work to finish, so we'll have to start a couple of hours later than usual, okay?"

Estelle nodded.

***

Stephen hid out in the basement pretending to be engrossed in work.

His watch lay abandoned on the work table but he checked it every twenty minutes. Upstairs, Estelle glanced at the clock every ten minutes.

At the stroke of eight, Estelle descended the stairs to the basement. Stephen started tinkering with the equipment as soon as he heard her footsteps. He did not look up as she emerged from the stairwell.

Estelle waited for a moment or two. "Stephen, we should leave now. It's already two hours past our usual time; it isn't fair to keep them waiting."

Stephen finally looked up. "Okay."

Estelle heaved a sigh of relief and pounded up the stairs yelling at Emily to bring herself and her bag downstairs.

Stephen started dragging his feet up the stairs, when the Earth tilted slightly. Stephen stared up at the door in alarm.

Had he imagined it?

Another tilt. This time his feet slipped out from beneath him and he was thrown backward off the stairs, landing at the foot of the stairwell in a heap.

Resounding crashes sounded above him, followed by screams. Stephen rolled onto his feet, wincing, and flew up the stairs, the shaking of the Earth threatening to throw him off every step of the way.

Panting, he stepped into the hall, just as a huge chunk of the ceiling came crashing down.

Emily screamed. Estelle sobbed.

Stephen did neither; he imprinted upon his vision, the sight of these two people, who were more precious to him than life itself.

As blackness overcame him, his only thought was, *perhaps this time I'll be lucky.*

To Fly
RubyPond

In air amidst a spread-wing length, I see
The freedom roll of land beneath my span
Where in the twilit sky—a destiny
    In air amidst a spread-wing length, I see
    A future of a life drawn out—'twould be
    A place where lies before us this great plan
        In air amidst a spread-wing length, I see
        The freedom roll of land beneath my span

To soar across a sky—like bird—be free
From all repressive thought that taunts a man
From mountaintop to mountaintop—agree
    To soar across a sky—like bird—be free
    A catalyst—my faith—the glue I'd need
    To raise me up to heights—I'd fly so grand
        To soar across a sky—like bird—be free
        From all repressive thought that taunts a man

Will catch a wind of hope—on bended knee
Then fly above all fears—this fate at hand
Take flight in spirit cast—my plight to be
    Will catch a wind of hope—on bended knee
    No burden—weighted down, pressed hard—a plea
    'twill fall before I rise and take my stand
        To catch a wind of hope—on bended knee
        Then fly above all fears—this fate at hand

And I, upon this wing—a mystery
Take to the sky and know who's in command
Review my triumphs made—my history
    For, I upon this wing—a mystery
    Take note the heights I climb—endeavored spree
    So far above the burdens of the land
        Though, I upon this wing—a mystery
        Take to the sky and know—who's in command

Whale Song

Matthew Harrison

Angie looked at the results from the Very Large Array with a growing sense of disquiet. Their project was getting attention from the big boys now, as well as priority funding, but too much attention was a danger.

When a small observatory like the Lick had such a prominent role in an international project like this, there were jealousies, things were said behind backs. The media too, needed careful handling; there was already a run of 'little green men' stories. Politicians were sniffing around, things could get out of control.

The report did not change what they already knew, but added the weight of confirmation. The signal they had spotted and tried to track with their limited scopes had been pinned down by the VLA, and refined by collation with other detectors. Its existence was now beyond doubt.

"The signal is an intermittent pulse," Angie read aloud from the report.

"Intermittent—that's one way to put it."

This comment came from her red-haired assistant Ross, who was almost leaning over her shoulder in that too-familiar way of his. Angie's husband Tom joked about "her young man", and it was more than a joke—the two of them had to work quite close together in the observatory, yet they were effective. Ross's breezy American manner counterpointed her British caution, leading to insights that neither of them could have managed alone.

It had been Ross who had spotted the signal which had drawn the attention of the world, but he was a pain.

Angie took a step away from her subordinate.

Oblivious, Ross went on. "Another way to put it would be, 'occasional', or, 'out to lunch'. I mean, sometimes there's a spike every few minutes, sometimes it's days with nothing. What kind of object is that?"

He looked at Angie quizzically, as if she were somehow responsible for the errant signal.

She would not let herself be provoked. "Whatever it is, it's in Cetus. The direction's nailed down."

"The original 'Little Green Men' radio pulses turned out to be rotating neutron stars," Ross mused almost to himself. "But no rotation can produce signals like these, they're too irregular. There's something weird going on here."

Angie was silent. They had discussed this many times.

"If you ask me," Ross continued unabashed, 'it seems almost like some kind of beacon. You know, an AI-enabled one-—sometimes off, sometimes on, sometimes urgent when someone is approaching. I don't suppose we're simply looking at one of our own satellites?"

"I would hope we know where those are," Angie said. "Now, stop speculating and do some scientific analysis. We need our best estimate on the distance, for Partington and the project board tomorrow."

Ross gave a mock salute and got down to work.

***

Angie left the observatory early and walked down to the parking lot just below the summit of Mount Hamilton. Cloud cover below masked the residual glare from San Jose, and overhead Angie could see the stars coming out.

Her experienced eye traced the constellations, faint though they were; in the west, setting into the sea, she spotted Cetus and stopped. Just a few evenings before, she had introduced the quaint whale of popular mythology to her children.

The whale was quaint no longer. Its quadrant of the sky held something—something they did not understand.

As she watched, the darkness grew and the dim stars gradually brightened. The faint smudge of the Milky Way became visible, indicating the vast scale of the cosmos through which their little world sailed, their observatory the minutest of lookouts on that vastness.

A breeze lifted the flaps of her jacket, and Angie shivered. Folding her arms across her chest, she trotted the last few yards into the lot, and with relief opened her car door.

That night, Angie played with Katie and her dolls on the floor, getting up now and then to encourage Brett to do his homework. Tom messaged from his seminar, her mother called, the dolls picked up dust from the floor, Brett threw his eraser at Katie. Even as she dealt with each of these small tugs at her attention, Angie's mind never left the signals. *What kind of object could generate such a pulse?* It was hard, as Ross said, to avoid thinking in terms of a beacon or some other artifact. Hard to avoid thinking of *intelligence.*

No, that was premature, unworthy of a scientist. She made herself focus on pouring the water for Katie's bath. As she soaped the soft body of her daughter—a body so small yet charged with the miraculous strength of life—her mind circled remorselessly around the question. *What evidence had been found for the existence of aliens?* It was precisely zero. That, of course, didn't mean alien life was non-existent; just that they hadn't been looking in the right place, or the right way. *Or with proper funding,* she thought grimly as she wiped Katie's back. *Science followed the money.*

By the time she heard Tom's key in the lock, the children were in bed and Angie was logged on to the observatory's net, checking Ross's results. They were no better than she had expected.

From the intensity of the signal, and known background factors, certain parameters could be drawn, but they were very broad. "It's basically anything from a nearby faint source, a few lightyears away, to a distant strong source perhaps hundreds of lightyears," she said ruefully to Tom as he came in to her room. "How can I tell the board that?"

"You're tired," he said, wrapping his arms around her shoulders. "Why don't you go to bed? It will look better in the morning."

Angie messaged Ross to stop for the night, and went up to the bedroom. At the window she paused, holding the curtains.

Here, the glare from the suburban streets drowned out the stars.

The brightly-lit neighbourhood demanded her attention—the local convenience store opposite, and the Cadillac that for some reason had pulled up outside. She tried to focus on these small things, seeing the Cadillac's driver through the store window buying something, the store owner's cap nodding, the minds of the two men no doubt filled with humdrum concerns about groceries, gas, payment. These were concerns of a humanity safe within its bubble of light and air. She too, proud though she was of her transition from the English Midlands to California, was in the greater scheme of things as small and preoccupied as those specimens of humanity opposite.

Angie shut the curtain, enclosing herself in the small room, with its cosy lamplight and comforting furnishings, feeling no comfort.

***

In the morning, she found an urgent message from Ross in her email. He had been working overnight, and he had a bombshell.

"I didn't want to wake you," he said. Angie cradled the phone against her shoulder as she got Katie ready for kindergarten. "But we think we've found an echo."

Angie, struggling to get Katie's arm into the sleeve of her blouse, could not at first get it. "An echo? From where?"

"From Eris."

"*What!?*" Angie stood stock still, unable to take it in. Part of her was aware that Tom took over Katie, and then returned to steer her gently to a seat at the dining table. But her mind was screaming, *Impossible!*

Rapidly, she turned over conjectures. The source was so faint that it had taken the VLA to confirm it; reflections of that source off the icy surface of Eris, the dwarf planet some ninety astronomical units away, would be hopelessly weak and scattered. Even if, somehow, an echo could be detected, Eris was too close to Earth to provide much parallax on a distant object. Her mind rattling through the possibilities, she said, "How does that help with triangulation?"

"A lot," came her assistant's cheery response. There was a pause.

"Go on," Angie said, calmer now. It must simply be a mistake.

Ross's chuckle came over the line. "We think the object's between Eris and us."

Angie was again too flabbergasted to respond. She gripped the wooden chair in her free hand, vaguely aware of Tom hovering anxiously.

At last she found her voice. "But that's *near*, Ross. Far too near. Are you sure?"

Ross, of course, was not sure. It was merely that an ongoing investigation of Eris had picked up what appeared to be the same signal as theirs. "It was much fainter, of course, and lagged just over an hour, which would be consistent with the object having a distance from us ..." he paused, " ... of eighty-one AU.

"We're checking, of course, it could be some artifact in the data. But we have more than one source. And the data goes back a while, just no one connected it to our project before."

The data goes back a while...?

"Yes," Ross continued, as if reading his boss's mind, "we can calculate the trajectory. Whatever it is, it's approaching us fast."

Angie, now in control of herself, barely felt this latest shock. "That means we might be able to see it. This is huge, Ross. You need to get time on Hubble, the Spitzer, anything!"

"Yes-sir! Actually, the James Webb's already on it. I'll see about others. Our Shane reflector's trying but it will be too faint." With that Ross rang off.

Angie refocused. Her family was staring at her from the breakfast table. As she tried to smile reassurance, Katie got down from her chair, ran round, and hugged Angie's knees, bursting into tears. Angie fondled Katie's hair, then picked her up. She sat the girl on her knee to finish breakfast.

"Just what is happening?" Tom asked, once the school bus had picked the children up.

Angie turned to her husband. She took in his anxious face, so strong and yet so vulnerable in the greater scheme of things. She took in the homely surroundings of their kitchen, Katie's rumpled cardigan, the dishes waiting in the sink—-the preoccupations of their little lives. Never had they seemed so precious, and yet so transient, compared with the vastness that was her daily preoccupation.

"We're expecting a visit," she said, trying to smile.

***

"We'll have time to put out the welcome mat!" was Partington's dry comment when Ross had finished. The grey-haired Project Director had listened through the presentation at their Santa Cruz headquarters unperturbed, as if he had seen it all before.

But he hasn't seen it before, Angie reminded herself. *No one has.*

Ross, however, gave the Director his due. "Our calculations, based on the increasing lag of the Eris subsidiary echo would be consistent with a speed of around fifty kilometers per second, which would bring the thing, whatever it is, into the inner solar system, by..." he paused.

"...by 2033," Partingdon completed the sentence for him. "So, E7055-351 won't arrive until eight years from now. After my retirement." He glanced smugly around the room.

"Hope it won't disrupt the golf," Angie heard Ross murmur. Aloud, her assistant stressed that the data was subject to checking, not to mention the uncertainty about the object itself. "I guess we shouldn't write it off to retirement just yet," he concluded wryly.

Partington gruffly took charge. The group went through the data sources and Ross's calculations, which even now were being refined, but the broad picture remained the same. Something that emitted sporadic signals was nearing Earth's orbit, and within a very short time—in astronomical terms—it would be upon them.

Angie thought of the public reaction, the possible panic, her own family. This was something huge for mankind. *And Partington is talking about retirement!* With difficulty she controlled herself.

Partington then switched to the signal itself. He had two questions.

What did the signal reveal about E7055, and what, if anything, did the signal signify? The group debated Ross's beacon idea without coming to any conclusion. Angie wondered if the signal could be some kind of code, like Morse; but then what to make of the long pauses between signals?

"They're Goddamn patient aliens, if they're content to send across three pips a day," Partington said scornfully. "And an interesting mix of technologies—interstellar transport and Morse code!"

Someone else said that the quality of the signal was strange. A machine-generated signal would combine multiple frequencies, and would have fuzziness around it from imprecision in the equipment. But the signal they were receiving was just a single spike in a very narrow frequency range.

The morning passed in unsatisfactory conjecture and counter-conjecture, and time was running out. Others had caught on to the data from the VLA; Ross was tracking blog commentary on his personal computer. Partington had to bow out of the meeting to join the communications group; they had scheduled a press conference for that afternoon, and then the National Security Council wanted a briefing.

"You take over," he said curtly to Angie as he left. "Get more facts. Only way to stop them biting our ass!"

Angie nodded, unsure where the facts were going to come from.

As Partington was stepping out of the door, the images came streaming in from the James Webb.

***

'Giant blob approaching!' screamed one headline on Ross's PC. 'Aliens communicate in code!' shouted another.

"Not bad," Ross said grudgingly as he scrolled through blogs and media sites. "Their guesses are no worse than ours."

It was the fifth day since the discovery of the echo. At Partington's suggestion, they had split into groups, and were working round the clock to brainstorm ideas.

He and another team tried to link in the efforts of the proliferating network of people working on what was now the global project of the day, while trying to manage the media and keep the politicians comfortable at the same time. *Retirement has obviously receded from the Director*, Angie thought, seeing his worn face over the video link, *as has sleep*. She almost felt sorry for him. The world was watching and demanding answers; there was no escaping the pressure.

Angie was going over the available data for the umpteenth time. Tom had just brought her a change of clothes, and a card from Katie which she received with a pang of guilt. She had been at the observatory continuously, sleeping on a camp bed in her office, phoning home once a day. Ross had a mattress on the operations floor. She had only seen him sleeping on it once; the young man seemed tireless.

Just as she thought this, her red-haired assistant leaned back from the screen and rubbed his eyes. "Got a message from my girlfriend," he said, his eyes still covered. "She was asking if I enjoy sleeping with my hot boss. I told her my boss was a mother of two, not hot.

"Just kidding," he added, looking at her now, provoking. "The not-hot comment..."

That was surely a breach of the observatory's code, but Angie saw the trembling of the lips, the shadows under the eyes; collapse was just a whisker away.

Briskly, she said, "Where have we gotten to?"

Ross blinked, and straightened in his seat. "E7055 is clear enough," he said in a firm voice. "At least, the latest visual image from the James Webb is clear. It's fifty milliarcseconds across, about three thousand clicks at that distance, larger than Eris or Pluto, but..."

Angie waited; she had seen the images too.

Ross struggled with it. "It's too *long*, Ange," he said at last, turning his screen towards her.

They both gazed at the improbable distended blob, still fuzzy at the limit of magnification. It was half again as wide as it was tall.

"How is that even possible?" Ross whispered.

Angie swallowed. "Gravity should make it round – something so massive. Or are we just not seeing its poles? Maybe an extremely low albedo?" Even as she spoke, she realized how desperate this sounded.

Ross shook his head. "There's a lot of heavy metal tracking this. And it's not just the professionals, the amateur reports are streaming in too, filling out the picture."

"Rotation?" Angie tried again.

They both checked, but rotation rapid enough to flatten such a massive sphere was also ruled out.

At a ping from Ross's PC, he turned the screen back to see what had come in. After a minute he lifted shocked eyes to her. "Take a look at this," he said huskily.

Angie snorted—they couldn't take too much more. She yanked the screen back from him, took a deep breath to steady herself, and read. The object had occulted a minor background star. She brightened; that would give them a better reading on its shape, at least in one dimension, but the report was curiously vague. *'Interpolations', 'Hiatuses', What was going on?*

Impatiently, she scrolled down. *Was it a flaw in the data?*

"It's got h–*holes?*" Ross stuttered.

The impossibility of a planet-sized mass holed like a piece of cheese hung in front of them. What physics would they have to abandon to embrace that?

Then Angie saw it. "E7055 is a cloud!" she cried triumphantly.

* * *

Her sense of triumph did not last; the cloud idea was swiftly taken up by the project community, and confirmed beyond doubt by further occultations, but the questions and conjectures that resulted were almost worse than when they had known less.

"We'll be wishing it was a planet after all!" Ross said ruefully.

Angie saw how his hair was no longer buoyant but matted around his head, and she knew how tired she must look, but this was a national, or more accurately an international, emergency. Mankind was being approached by something they did not understand; they had to carry on.

Once again, they pored over the signal charts. There had been some two thousand spikes over the past month, sometimes fifty or more at fixed intervals of minutes each, sometimes nothing for a day or two, then another string at longer intervals. As she strained to make out patterns, Angie found the charts blurring. She closed her eyes and turned away.

They had to find the answer, and she wasn't setting a good example. Pulling herself together, she tried again, "Do you think that there is an underlying signal which is more regular, just that it's getting blocked from time to time by something in between?"

"No," Ross said. Too tired for joviality, he explained, "The echo matches the source. Any blocking factor would interfere more with one signal than the other, creating a difference. But there isn't one."

Angie realised dully she should have thought of that. Rising, she pulled her coat off the chair and said she was going to get some air.

Outside, the sky was mercifully covered in high clouds, and she looked at the bounded world of San Francisco Bay, with its towers and lights and the thread-like structure of its bridges in the distance. From this mountaintop it was remote, but it was unchanged. Humanity was still there, largely oblivious to their discoveries. Taking comfort, Angie drew her coat around her and walked back indoors.

Ross, meanwhile, seemed to have revived, and with a hint of his former gaiety, he confided in Angie that he had played around with the signal a bit. "Actually, I converted it to audio – audible range, of course." As Angie stared, he brought up the file on his PC, and clicked it on.

Angie heard the almost imperceptible hiss of feedback, then came the 'Plunk' of the spike, followed by near-silence. The seconds passed, one minute, then two. The office's ticking clock obtruded on her numbed consciousness. Three minutes. Finally, another, 'Plunk'.

"That's real time. Now, if you speed it up..." Ross tapped the screen, and after a shorter interval came a higher-pitched, 'Plink'. He ratcheted up the frequency so that Angie heard a still higher-pitched, 'Pip...Pip... Pip' before it passed the threshold of her hearing.

Ross grinned. "Let's keep it in the audible spectrum." He fiddled with the tools, then sat back. "I've dialed it down about twenty octaves," he explained. "Listen." He pressed Play.

The sound issuing from the speaker was totally unexpected. Angie listened to the warbling hooting notes that rose and fell and rose again. Unmistakable, familiar. She smiled.

"And it had to be in Cetus," Ross said softly.

***

It was Partington, of course, who took the glory. The Project Director dominated the press conference, explaining how they had cracked the alien code––*although it probably wasn't a code at all,* Angie thought wryly, *but communication in clear*––by converting the electromagnetic signals received on Earth, into sound.

"The message starts as sound waves in the cloud," Partington explained to the intrigued audience, "creating local compressions that give rise to electromagnetic signals. We take these EM signals, and convert them back to sound waves again." At his nonchalant signal, Ross put on his tape; as the warbling notes filled the auditorium, the audience fell into a gaping silence. Then came the tumult of questions.

***

It was towards the end of the afternoon when they had gotten rid of the final journalist. Ross had commissioned balloons in E7055's blob shape with added whale fins and flukes, and these proved popular as takeaways.

That is a young man who will go far, Angie thought, as she picked up a couple for her children. *And the farther the better.*

She waved to Partington, as the director gave the team a last thumbs-up before disappearing into a limousine with the bigwigs.

Angie walked slowly down to the observatory lawn, where Tom and Katie were waiting. There followed a family hug, which had to be repeated when Brett returned with his ice cream. The whale balloons proved a hit.

Later, when the children scampered off to the small telescope overlooking the bay, she and Tom were left standing together.

"So we've got eight years," he said.

"Is it enough?" Angie looked into her husband's eyes.

Tom laughed, raised a bemused hand to his face, dropped it again. "I guess . . . I don't know. It's such a crazy thing, Ange. How can we get used to their pace? Slow down that much?"

"I don't think we can," Angie said. Having lived with the signals for so long, she had thought it through. "We are quick-living creatures. If the signals are really what we think, and if you scale up from what seem to be messages and project estimates in terms of whales, their lives would last hundreds of thousands of years. There's no way we can relate to that. To us, it's the span of a species, not of an individual."

She gestured toward the bay, its blocks and towers a mere crust on the green slopes at this distance, faint in the winter sunshine. "For them, the entire development of this city would be a conversation's length. For them, Columbus arrived a month ago, humans reached the bay a year back. If they lived here, they would have seen the ice rise and cover the bay and retreat, again and again. Maybe they have been by, aeons ago."

"What interest would they have in us?"

"Maybe not much." Angie sighed. "To them, we would be less than mayflies—flitting about with our frenzied plans, scheming, toiling, loving, fighting, the whole damn dance, and then gone, almost before they were aware of us. We don't know if they are intelligent, in the human sense—or even if they're a *they*. Maybe what we're detecting is just a single entity talking to itself."

Tom laughed uneasily again. "Hmm. Travelling for aeons through space talking to yourself. I'm not sure *I* would have anything to say to a being like that."

The sun sank behind the clouds, and the bay with its little crust of human artifacts became dull grey. Cold was stealing in from the hills. Angie shivered. With the cold came hunger—hunger for the dance that drove all living things forward in their frenetic race.

Angie called to the children, then turned to Tom. "Tell me honestly—am I hot?"

Before her startled husband could answer, she seized him in her arms and hugged him so tightly he could hardly breathe.

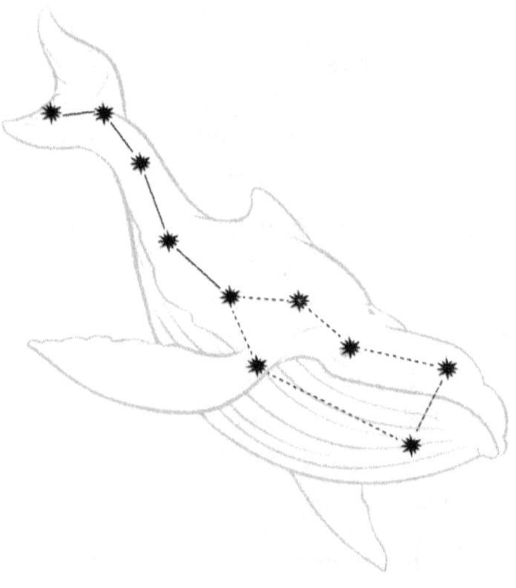

Color-Coded & Iridescent
Megan Denese Mealor

You dress in dogwood rose,
claret, jungle green;
chisel Chinese violet
out of bones and ebony.

I found a scribbled sonnet
inside your june bud jeans,
saw the way you danced in Venice,
your lines a sleek, sweet cream.

Your eyes could be a landscape,
its sky every shade of blue.
The instant when your heart stood still:
the most fuchsia part of you.

(ORIGINALLY PUBLISHED IN OBSESSED WITH PIPEWORK, SPRING 2014)

Charcoal
Angela L. Lindseth

Personal log 04/04/2163

The pinging that brought us to this sector of the galaxy is coming from a Spector-18 exploratory vessel, old, but still used in some quadrants. It's unknown how long the ship has been adrift. No references to its identification number have been found in our ship's databases, but our records only go back a hundred years.

There are no obvious signs of distress, and the body of the vessel is intact.

Mooring cables are in place, and an exploratory survey of the exterior is scheduled for tomorrow.

Personal log 04/05/2163

We have discovered a peculiar powdery substance on the exterior of the hull. Bobby took scrapings of the gray and black scale; sample analysis indicates severe carbonation. Dating of the material eliminates the possibility of an Earth origin, and the thickness of the scales indicates it formed after the craft became immobile. The engineers haven't yet come up with a viable explanation for its development in deep space.

Personal log 04/06/2163

We have been observing the ship for two days, per protocol, and have not discovered any signs of life. Motion detectors, heat imaging, and audio recordings have all been negative.

Preparations have been made for the Lead Engineer's Alpha-boarding in the morning.

Personal log 04/07/2163

Bobby entered alone through the aft portal to conduct the Alpha monitoring. He took all the required initial entry readings and samples. Standard operating procedures for boarding abandoned craft were followed. Full-body protective gear was worn.

I monitored his live video feed. Nothing peculiar stuck out to me. No sign of the crew—they seemed to have literally vanished.

Analysis of the samples failed to raise any red flags. All parameters were within acceptable limits, and Beta-boarding will be initiated in the morning.

At dinner tonight, Bobby complained about numbness in his fingertips which struck me as odd. It's not like him to complain or express discomfort.

Personal log 04/08/2163

Beta-boarding teams consisted of: Team 1- myself, Bobby, and Raj; Team 2 - Shannon, Marco, and Sherman. Our team was responsible for reconnaissance and overall assessment. Team 2 was responsible for establishing the vessel's operability.

Team 1 conducted a sweep of all three levels. Our primary mission was to determine why the Spector-18 was abandoned, and what had happened to the crew. We found no signs of distress, but we did find numerous piles of an ashy material, and a thin film of the carbon substance, similar to the piles, covered most surfaces. We collected samples of these materials and food supplies. We discovered some dry goods, but no liquids of any sort.

Team 2 was able to restore the craft's life support systems. Computers are now back online, but the memory files are oddly corrupted and have been no help in determining why the ship was abandoned. I've ordered the crew to maintain protective precautions until further notice.

Bobby worked this morning, but after I noticed him flexing and shaking his hands, I sent him back to our ship for a medical examination.

Personal log 04/09/2163

I sent two crews to conduct a thorough inspection of the Spector's lower decks today. They reported more of the gritty piles. Analysis of the substances shows it is composed of nearly pure carbon. The piles, the film on most of the surfaces, and the scale on the hull are all the same. Its origin is unknown, and I've made solving this mystery our highest priority.

Update on Bobby: He's experiencing numbness in his toes, and considerable decreased mobility in his fingers. Doc Peters hasn't been able to figure out the cause yet; there are no symptoms other than the numbness and a slight fever.

Personal log 04/10/2163

Shannon and Marco both mentioned numbness in their fingers today. Bobby's illness is spreading up his arms, and his toes and feet are now showing signs of atrophy as well. He claims he feels no pain, even though his fingers are the color of shale. Doc says he's drinking an inordinate amount of water.

It's unclear if the Spector-18 is causing these symptoms, but it seems likely.

Personal log 04/11/2163

Bobby's condition severely degraded during the night. His fingers and arms have turned black, brittle and cracked, and they radiate heat. He accidently knocked his hand against the counter, and his pinky and ring finger broke off. He said there was no pain, but fear shone bright in his eyes. I've ordered him quarantined, along with Shannon and Marco, but if this is an airborne infection, I'm afraid it may be too late to stop the spread.

Shannon and Marco's conditions have also deteriorated; however, Marco's feet have decayed faster and he can no longer stand, for fear of them breaking off.

I ordered recalibration of all our instruments and a secondary run of tests, full spectrum, but they revealed nothing. It's too late to abandon our mission especially since we haven't determined a cause of the contagion.

We used every instrument to test the air, but we must have missed something. I don't know how else to explain it. Hell, I don't know; maybe we absorbed something subatomic. It seems the piles of ash on the Spector-18 are no longer a mystery, but I hate to imagine the implications.

I've sent messages out any neighboring ships, but I don't expect an answer. This is what we signed up for. Downloads of ship's activities are sent back to Earth every day, but the lag time in responses is twenty-seven days, and any attempted rescue would take years.

I don't think we have that much time.

Starting to worry about our water supply.

Personal log 04/12/2163

The effects of the virus—or whatever the hell it is—hit Raj, Sherman and four others who never even stepped foot on the Spector-18. It's an alarming development, considering we took all decontamination precautions when traveling between ships.

Doc Peters is baffled. We're in agreement the contagion must be somehow caused by the carbon, although there's no direct evidence of the correlation. I haven't mentioned our conclusion to the crew, but they're not stupid. It's easy enough to connect the dots.

Bobby's in bad shape.

Me and Bobby go way back, all the way back to the academy. It's hard to watch him disintegrate. His body temperature has spiked to 112º, and it's impossible to keep him hydrated.

He drifts in and out of consciousness. His clothes smolder and spontaneously combust; little patches ignite revealing black and cracked skin. He lies immobile, but smoldering chunks of him spall away from his limbs. I'm not sure if he's aware, but he must be able to smell and see the smoke.

I see no reason to bring it up.

Personal log 04/13/2163

Five more showing symptoms. The medical bay is overflowing, and Doc Peters has locked himself in the lab. His assistant lost the use of his hands, so I help him out when I can. Mostly, he lets me bring him meals, but I usually take it away untouched. He sits hunched over the microscope muttering. He's taking it hard, and I worry about his stability.

Personal log 04/14/2163

I'm the only one left symptom-free; I feel like a traitor. The few who can still help, nurse the ones who've collapsed. They say the pain is minimal, but their thirst is unquenchable. I've rationed our water supplies, and the moans for more water haunt what little sleep I've been getting.

Doc Peters gave a little speech today, that ended with him distributing a pill to each of us. He plans on using his when his hands freeze up. He suggested we all consider the same. He's run out of options, ideas, and hope.

I could have shoved it down his throat and saved him the wait, because his 'pep talk' was unbecoming for a senior officer. On the other hand, some of the crew looked relieved to have an easier way out.

I cancelled all duties, and some of the crew have isolated themselves in their quarters. I can imagine them staring at the pill, gathering the nerve to use it.

I threw mine in the trash.

I am the captain. It's my duty to see this through to the end, and record every detail.

Personal log 04/15/2163

I'm showing the first signs of numbness.

I had hoped I was immune; witnessing my team turn into blackened statues and their appendages snap off like dead wood . . . well, horrific is hardly the word for it. We still haven't found a cure.

How can one discover an antidote without a diagnosis?

I make the rounds checking on everyone and noting their condition. I force myself to visit Bobby. He's lost the ability to talk, but he licks his lips over and over. I drip water into his mouth, but it's never enough. I can't look him in the eye. I don't know how much more I can take.

Personal log 04/16/2163

Doc Peters took his life today.

Personal log 04/17/2163

My progressive decay fascinates me. Like watching embers in a fire that move and wane, the degeneration works its way up my limbs. It's mesmerizing. The onset reminded me of a bad sunburn, but then the pain subsided to a dull ache and numbness took over.

I thought there might have been an explanation that didn't involve the Spector-18, but that's stupid. We were on a foreign vehicle, in an underexplored galaxy—I mean, how do you prepare for every unknown?

I am smoldering. My temperature is 105º, pulse rate is 53 bpm. Blood pressure 80/50. I should be dead. I wish I was.

The ship has grown quiet. I switched over to my thought recorder before paralysis is total. I wonder when that will be.

I wish I hadn't thrown away my pill.

Personal log 04/18/2163

The invader consumes with hot determination. The lucky ones crumbled to ash when they toppled, but some continue to twitch and moan where they made their last resting place. I ignore them the best I can. I guess I should put them out of their misery, but somehow I still have hope they will revive and grow their limbs back. It's ludicrous, I know, but I don't want to be out here alone and lost in this godforsaken place.

I experimented knocking my hand against something solid. My fingers shattered painlessly into charcoal briquettes. My hope flees with every minute.

Today my pulse rate is 42 bpm. Blood pressure 80/30. My temperature is 112º. I don't feel ill, but my thirst is unquenchable, and I've run out of water. My tongue protrudes from my mouth. My lips feel like sandpaper.

Personal log 04/21/2163

I'm forgetting my daily posts. I'm not even sure what day it is. I converted ship functions to automatic yesterday—at least I think it was yesterday. I imagine the last person 'alive' on the Spector-18 went through the same motions.

My temperature is an alarming 121º. My breath leaves my nostrils with tiny puffs of smoke. How is this even possible? I can feel my heart beat; the minimal tempo vibrates down my solidifying tissues like drum beats in the distance.

I shuffled around the laboratory on what is left of my legs pretending to work on a cure, pretending to have hope. I can't find any of Doc's pills. Maybe the last of the crew took them, and it didn't work. What a cruel joke.

Personal log 04

I can't move anymore. Hopefully, someone will find my thought recordings and process these messages before it happens to them.

If we are ever found.

How my heart beats in this blackened shell and supplies blood to my organs is all I think about, at least when I'm conscious.

I'm losing chunks of time, I think. Time passes like minutes and an eternity, at the same time.

For my final gesture, I toppled over across from the blackened husk of Bobby's body. What's left of him is on the floor of the isolation cell.

He's not moving. At first I thought he was dead, but his eyes locked on mine, alive and alert.

My God.

Log entry

Breathing . . . a chore.

Bobby's eyes . . . not blinking . . .

but once in a while . . . dart upward . . .

pleading to God . . .

If Bobby . . . alive . . .

he was first . . .

How long . . .

have I been here?

Professor Marvel
Richard King Perkins II

Natural order is chaos.
An invocation to your automaton power
brings saviors abounding in many forms,
freeing us temporarily
from the bondage of mechanical servitude.

Cogs of momentum claim everything
in the path of a thoughtless reaper.
Look for meaning in the eye
of every dark cloud
if it brings a passing comfort.

Pay no attention to that man
behind the curtain.
Every god will be revealed
as a well-intentioned charlatan
over the course of unending time.

A Diamond In The Sky
RubyPond

Kneeling, Ferren the Platen reached over the fallen female Gadis, her shiny braids of pink silk spilling in waves across the rock beneath her. He repeatedly grasped the empty space over her, frantically hoping for traces of absom. The more frantically he grasped, the more worried he got. Absom was the essence of life on Gadendonia—like air on Earth. He was almost panicking now.

Wait! There it was. A tiny vibration in his right pinky. It was ever so slight, yet unmistakable. Sweat began to bead around his brow and he steadied himself on his knees. Spreading his fingers, he focused his full concentration on the energy he felt in his pinky.

There it was again. A small vibration.

"Come on damn it..." he muttered under his breath. His breastplate squeezed as he leaned in this awkward position; he knew he couldn't hold it for much longer. "Come on! Absom! Absom!" His voice quivered from the strain. He was about to fall when a ripple of electricity shot through his arm, into his breastplate, and threw him back.

He scrambled to his feet and watched a circle of energy spread like a cloud across the Gadis, engulfing her. She lay with her eyes closed, lips slightly parted, unaware that she was being returned to life, nor that she had ever died.

Ferren stood and watched in silence, admiring the work of the universe, only now understanding the love he felt for this being who lay barely breathing, but she WAS breathing! He watched as her delicate wrists and long fingers began to twist and move and grasp at the air. First slowly, and then desperately as she became more conscious. Her tall slender body was rising, slightly levitating into the energy as she wrestled to gain control. He watched the aura encircle her like an electric cloud, lifting and vibrating her body as she flailed her arms and kicked her legs.

At last, a cough and her eyes slowly opened. Iridescent beams bled out of them, tracking back and forth with changing hues as she took in her field of vision.

It was difficult to look straight at her. He had always been taught to never look a Gadis in the eye lest he be blinded. Only temporarily, but a warrior could not chance even a temporary blindness.

In full animation now, the Gadis rose in all her glory, and as the aura dissipated, her feet commanded the ground beneath her to hold her towering female form erect. The rays of light from her eyes, now a rainbow of fluorescence digitally scanning the surrounding area, caught Ferren by surprise when they settled on him.

He knew the procedure though. He closed his eyes and stood still, allowing her to process his being—to scan his shape and take him in. He felt the hair on his neck rise in reaction, yet he rested in the familiarity of her intake, and breathed a sigh of relief, knowing now she would be okay.

"Dardvor! It is I, Ferren! Are your algorithms registering properly? Do you recognize me?" Ferren shifted through the air in his humanistic habit, appearing to walk as a man, yet his feet never actually touched the ground. His royal blue bodysuit, clad to a muscular human form, swished with the movement gracefully. His breastplate firmly squeezed his midsection and holding it stiff, guarded his vital organs and intricate brain.

As he moved closer to the Gadis, Dardvor robotically shifted her head toward him, lowering her eyes so as not to blind him—a sign that she recognized him. Her beautiful full lips spread slightly, and two ivory tipped fangs slipped momentarily from the corners of her mouth, then receded almost immediately. It was a normal facial movement, one Ferren recognized as a friendly greeting.

"Ferren! What happened?" Dardvor dazed, looked to her Platen friend. Ferren was unlike other Platens. He was friendly and compassionate. Though a warrior through and through, he had characteristics different than others from Platenia. When Platenia invaded Gadendonia, they had been caught off guard; the Gadendonians were nearly annihilated, along with many of the Platens.

There were now only a little over a thousand of her species left.

The Platens had brought genetic time capsules from three other planets: Botmou, Uvasia, and Crictmior. All these time capsules contained lifeform DNA from each planet. Platen scientists mixed and harvested the DNA from the test tubes, forming one superior race they called Absomolites, and they renamed the planet Absomethia.

Although the Platens were intellectually superior, they were soon outnumbered and overrun by their creations. As things went wildly awry, the Absomolites became more and more unmanageable. Still enemies with the Platens, the Gadendonians had gathered in underground caves and adapted to living in the depths of the planet, in order to remain hidden.

A few of the Platens objected to the hierarchy and had separated from the rest; Ferren was one of these. He and his tribe cohabited an underground cave with the Gadendonians. Some of them even formed friendships, and frequently the female Gadendonians—the Gadis—formed close relationships with the male Platens. The Gadons, or male Gadendonians, were not happy about this, so these relationships were kept secret unless and until they were dedicated to each other permanently. Unable to find a mate, or merely discouraged at the reduction in choices, many of the Gadons would return to the Absolomites.

"Come! Let's take cover and I will explain!" Ferren said as he led Dardvor into the bushes and through the entrance to an underground tunnel. As they entered, Ferren turned, squeezed his fists together, and aimed them at a nearby boulder. The rock shook but did little more than that.

"Here, let me help." Dardvor pushed her fists together like Ferren, and both concentrated on the boulder. The huge rock rumbled and shook, and finally rolled two turns across the entrance of the cave. Darkness closed in with the exception of the colorful beams coming from Dardvor's eyes. One of the great qualities first recognized by the Platens, was the ability of Gadendonians to provide light—and the need for light was great underground.

"I see your full strength is back," said Ferren. "Thank goodness! I thought I'd lost you. You were out in that damn field again! What have I told you about that?

"A troop of Absomolites stumbled across you. You tried to run, but they zapped you with a taser. You flipped through the air at least thirty times and slammed against the rock. Then you just fell silent. You had no aura, no absom! I thought you were dead!"

Ferren touched her shoulder and looked down, a loving gesture, established between the two races to replace looking into each other's eyes, since that would mean at least a severe burn to the cornea of the Platen. "You have to promise me that you won't wonder so far out there again. I know you like to stargaze and create, but it is just too dangerous!"

"I know, and I will be careful, but you know I won't stop. It is the only thing that makes me happy." She raised her forearm across her brow, a sign of embarrassment. "Thank you for saving me."

Stargazing and creating was a hobby only a few Gadendonians took to; there were only a few with the raw talent to make it worth the time. Dardvor was one of these extremely talented individuals. The elders knew she was gifted, from the time she was a small kidling.

Her hobby was something she did with her eyes. She would sit alone in a field, staring intently at the stars in the sky, and as she concentrated she would focus her eyes on one small star. The harder she stared and concentrated, the more energy she would radiate toward the star, and soon the star would begin to react and divide. All Gadendonians could do this, but only the extremely talented ones—like Dardvor—could then bend those stars into beautiful shapes, like crystals in the sky.

Once she was through creating, Dardvor would name her star design, and with the natural laser beams in her eyes, she would weave a signature emblem across the surface of the star, unique to the artist, identifying it as hers. Dardvor had 40 or more star creations with her signature on them.

"Dardvor, I want to ask you something." Farren lifted his forearm to his brow, more than a little nervous. "We have been friends for several months now, and you have become very important to me." He hesitated, and once again lifted his forearm to his brow. Dardvor lifted her forearm to her brow as well. One small fang slipped from the corner of her crooked smile, and quickly receded.

"This is more difficult than I imagined. Ugh!" Ferrin slid smoothly across the floor of the cave in front of Dardvor, almost touching his feet to the ground. Together, they both moved their forearms across their brows. "You must know that I am in love with you by now!" Both forearms now simultaneously touched each side of his brow, signifying the most intense embarrassment.

Dardvor giggled slightly, and she too raised both forearms to her brow. "I know, I feel the same." She touched his shoulder and cast her eyes to the ground.

"Will you be my accompiant?" This was a term used to define a female or male partner, who had promised to devote themselves to each other for eternity, to become mates and reproduce, if it were possible and allowed between their species.

Ferren touched her shoulder and cast his eyes downward. He resisted the urge to touch forearm to brow again, as he nervously waited for her response.

"Oh, Ferren! This is a day I have longed for! Yes!"

Ferren knelt, levitated in the air an inch off the ground, and circled her in three slow sequential ringlets, symbolizing the joining together of their souls, as they both cast their eyes down in adoration of each other. This was traditional after an accompiant engagement, and it sealed their unity and vow to be joined together.

He rose to his feet, and as he touched her left shoulder, she touched his right; they stood together this way for what seemed like hours, eyes cast downward, enjoying the union of their love.

"Shall we go tell the others?" Ferren asked her.

"Yes! But, first let me stargaze and create a star just for us!" She could see he was hesitating. "I really must! Please? You can come with me!"

Ferren could hear the excitement in her voice, and knew it was useless to resist. He reasoned he would be able to protect her, since he would be of little interest to the Absomolites. Platens usually had little to fear from the creatures, especially when a Gadendonian was present.

When a Platen was captured, there was a formal procedure that had to take place before they could be arrested or killed, since not all Platens had separated from the social hierarchy; this was such a bother the Absomolites usually would not waste their time, and the Platen would fair rather well with little to no harm. Farren took this into consideration, then prepared to guard his lovely accompiant as she paid tribute to their love in the stars.

The two of them joined forces, removed the boulder from the entrance of their cave, and returned to the field. Ferren followed at a close distance, keeping his awareness up, trying to make sure no one saw them. His hope was at the first sign of danger, he could clasp her in his grip and shoot them both through the air to safety. Dardvor was wandering aimlessly it seemed, with her head in the clouds, almost unaware of his presence. Then she stopped.

"That's it Ferren!" She pointed above her head. "That will be our star! I will call it 'Diamond in the Sky'"

She stiffened her body and entered a trance like state, eyes focused and shooting bright phosphoric lasers into the sky. Ferren looked from a sideways glance, so as not to burn his corneas, and for a moment he was lost in the brilliance of the lights.

He barely noticed the three Absomolites behind him, until it was too late. Before he could clutch Dardvor in his arms, they had her on the ground.

He felt his breastplate tighten and a force around his neck caused him to strain, merely to breathe. The squeezing against his brain made him dizzy. He watched helplessly as one of them stood over Dardvor and held her to the ground, while another drew its taser and blasted her between her eyes.

Dardvor almost seem to crumple and the light grew dim in her eyes. As the Absomolites moved away, Ferren watched her eyes go completely dark. Frantically, he grasped the air over her body, opening and closing his fist. Punching the air and running his fingers through what seemed like invisible material.

Even as he panicked and grasped, he knew there would be no absom this time.

She could not survive the impact between her eyes, centered on her main power source—her light had been extinguished for good.

As he mourned over her limp body, a sensation rose from underneath and seem to bring him downward. He felt the ground beneath his feet for the first time.

In utter grief, his levitation had failed him, and lowered him to the ground. The cold rock beneath his flesh made his bones ache and grieve, and he cast his eyes into the sky in the truest tribute to grief known to the Platens.

Emptiness embodied him.

As he soaked in the iciness of the barren ground through the souls of his feet, and let the sky pour sadness into his innards, a twinkling caught his attention.

There in the sky, hung the beautiful star with the signature emblem of his love, his lovely accompiant Dardvor, in the shape of a diamond with a circle through the middle. As he gazed upward, the star grew brighter and brighter, until he could no longer gaze at it.

He cast his eyes to the ground in adoration of his lost love, and his feet rose to an inch of levitation, while his breastplate squeezed his palpating heart and swaddled his aching soul.

He felt the heat from the brilliant star touch his shoulder, and he knew that their love would go on forever, in "The Diamond in the Sky".

In the Clouds
Lynn White

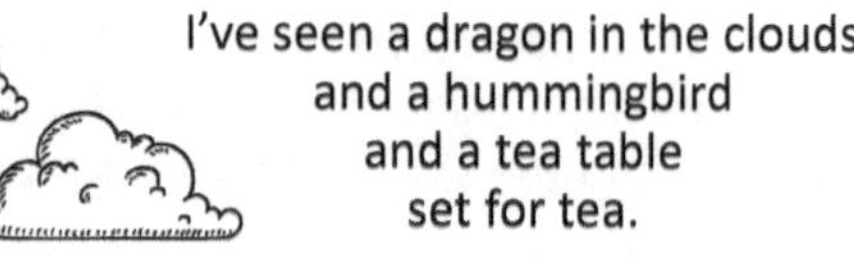

I've seen a dragon in the clouds
and a hummingbird
and a tea table
set for tea.

Some say they've seen Christ
or Mohamed,
or fairy kings and queens.
They have all stayed a while,
my shapes in the cloud.
None have left.
Not until now.

Now,
when I saw the man
with his tufts of hair
growing haphazardly
here and there.

With his open red mouth already blooded.
With the sunlight shining through his eyes.
I have never seen such colours in the clouds.

And now
he seems to be leaving,
not blown away,
but stepping out
looking
hungrily towards me.

Fuel Me Once

Allen Lang

"Alma, this Bloody Mary is Nobel Prizeworthy."

The young woman polished an empty glass with her bar towel. "Thank you, sir. I'll get to meet the King of Sweden then, and the medal will go nicely with this blouse."

"Most places you order a Bloody Mary, you get what looks like nosebleed. Yours is properly tawny." Mark Poinsette lowered his big-hatted head to address his drinking straw. He puckered and smiled. "Floats like a butterfly, stings like a bee."

"An apt quotation, sir."

The stranger to Mark's left raised a finger. "Miss Alma, I think I'll have what this gentleman is drinking."

"Indeed, sir."

The stranger stuck out his hand. "Derrick Drugar."

"Mark Poinsette." He took the stranger's hand. "Our Alma here, is the Marie Curie of bartenders, Mr. Drugar."

"Derrick."

"Mark."

Alma retired to her laboratory at the far end of the bar. She measured, whirred her electric mixer and then returned to place a tall glass before Derrick. He dipped his head and took a sip. "Oh, wow!"

"It bites you, then apologizes for having bitten you`," Mark said.

"Horseradish," Derrick said, licking his lips.

Alma smiled. "You have discerning taste buds, sir."

"Thank you. Now I'll trouble you for a glass of water, please. With ice."

"At once, sir."

"Haven't seen you in here before," Mark said.

"In town on business. I'm in the hydraulic-fracking game."

"That sounds like the punchline of a joke you wouldn't tell in front of Miss Alma. You frackin' after oil?"

"I frack for gas," Derrick said.

"I made my stake in petroleum," Mark said. "Oklahoma. Not so easy to find the stuff these days. No more Oklahomas. Got to bust through polar ice or poke holes in the bottom of the sea."

Derrick sucked up a bit more of his drink. "Whew! Like tapping into a geyser," he said. He had an ice water wash. "I tell you Mark, what us fossil-fuel folks gotta do, is discover your new Oklahoma."

"You know something I don't?"

"Yeah. I know I'm talking too much."

"Talk on," Mark said.

Derrick took two twenties from his billfold and set his empty glass atop them. "Had dinner? "We could talk oil over steaks."

"If you're buying," Mark said.

"I'm easy," Derrick said.

***

Après steak, their plates mopped clean, the men fortified their espressos with shots of Greek brandy.

"As I understand it, fracking is just cracking rocks underground," Mark said. "Then you squirt soapy water into the hole. Like givin' the Earth an enema."

"You understand physics pretty good."

"I get roughage. What did you mean about finding new oil?"

Derrick leaned over the table. "What would you say to a Great Lakes of gasoline?"

"I'd say, No Smoking."Derrick reached into the inner left pocket of his jacket to produce two objects in parchment sheaths. He handed one to his companion. "Cuban. No Customs stamp." He produced his lighter. Under merging clouds of smoke he asked, "Have you heard of Titan?"

"A brand of prophylactics," Mark said.

"It's a moon of Saturn," Derrick said.

"That planet that wears a hula hoop?"

"You know astronomy," Derrick said.

"I read the papers."

"Well, Mark, scientists have discovered that Titan is bellybutton-deep with polycyclic aromatic hydrocarbons."

"Do tell."

"That's gasoline, Mark. A Great Lakes of gasoline. Think of it. Billions, maybe even trillions of barrels, just waiting for us to slurp 'em up."

"That gasoline is a long way off."

His companion raised a finger. "True, our lakes of Titanic gasoline are pretty far away."

"Too far for a pipeline," Mark said. "You'd need tankers. Interplanetary tankers."

"You grasp the answer right away." Derrick shook his head. "What we need is a pump-primer. Capital to build your fleet of interplanetary supertankers."

Mark wafted a halo of cigar smoke toward the ceiling lights. Then he put his elbows on the table to lean closer to Derrick. "You're talking big money," he said.

"Peanuts." Derrick said. He reached into the right inner pocket of his jacket to fish out an olive-colored sheet of paper, folded to fit. He opened it.

"Signed by the Administrator of NASA," he said. "Highly confidential." He pushed the document across the table.

"License to import from Titan not more than ten million barrels of liquid hydrocarbons per annum, starting January next year."

"The Saudis won't be happy when we put our sky gas on the market," Mark said.

"Our?"

"Of course, 'Our.' You don't think I'd let an opportunity like this slip through my fingers," Mark said.

"So you're in?"

"Darn right," Mark said.

"How much can you put up to get our project started?"

"Bupkis," Mark said.

"What the devil do you mean?"

"I mean Zilch, Mister Derrick Drugar," Mark said. "I mean, either I call the cops to manacle and Miranda you for promoting the craziest con scheme any grifter ever came up with…" Mark paused "…or you make me your Marketing Director."

"Marketing Director?"

"And full partner. You've been thinking retail, Derrick. You don't want one rich old fool like me. What you want—what *we* want—is a whole swarm of cockroach capitalists begging us to accept their money to let them dip their beaks into our sky-juice," Mark said.

"Mark, you're not as dumb as you look," Derrick said.

Mark grinned. "Hardly anybody is, Partner."

The Clepostrum
Carl Nelson

Row upon row of Jahrvenskool interns
in cerulean blue uniforms of the Certainty
prowl the incoming biodata in real time,

picking through the flood
of call and response wave signatures,

looking for bullying, harassment,
and microaggressions

in a twenty-fifth century version
of the 'broken windows policy'.

Above the glowing monitors,
another monitor surveys
the student workers.

Attentional lapses spike a bright yellow,
graduating to orange for straying thought.

Sexual flashes light up the supervisor's screen
like fireflies.

'Humans and technology
in the twenty-fifth century

are proving to be like oil and water',
the supervisor sighs.

As a volunteer archivist
with a penchant for history,

she has been reading some of the
forbidden literature
of the twentieth century--

a necessity prior to archival--
and she wonders if perhaps

the simple nuclear family
weren't a better way
of shaping human behavior

than occipital chargers
and chromo pills.

But the idea of a husband...

how odd!

Perquisition
T. D. Kohler

Six Flags, New Orleans, LA
October 24, 2017 - 1921 hours

The clouds loom and slowly roll over each other, as a full moon peeks out to light up the grounds and the abandoned rides of what is left of Six Flags. The flood waters from Hurricane Katrina have long subsided, leaving the rides with a mossy, damp feel as they lay in ruins. Night critters scurry in and out of the equipment and electrical control panels, when a set of young voices can be heard in the distant background.

Unable to discern what the voices are saying, Gerald Malcolm lies on his back in the murk of the park, trying to shield his eyes from the moonlight with his arm. Struggling to summon the strength to call for help, he remains motionless, focusing on the voices. Information about the voices comes to him like data from a computer readout, printing out in his thoughts.

One soul 21 years, two souls 22 years, one soul 19 years. He lets out a soft moan, briefly stopping the mental printout. The printout continues. *Four souls 1 year, one soul 3 years.* Before he can comprehend this information, he hears a faint commotion in the near distance. Still unable to move, he feels something press up against his leg, but he is unable to see what it is.

His skin ripples, and a burning heat in his leg causes him to whip up into a sitting position. His skin starts to settle, and his mind begins to replay the commotion he heard a few seconds ago.

Large red eyes reflect the moonlight as I turn, and they lock me in place for a split moment. Terror overwhelms me, but before I can get to cover, flashes of claws come from out of nowhere; claws come from everywhere I try to turn. Searing pain, as the claws rip into my side and I am lifted off of the ground, into something hard, metallic.

I struggle to breathe but as I get to my feet, the claws are back. They land on my back, knocking me back down, pressing me to the ground. I cannot lift my head. I cannot see. I can't breathe.

Grabbing his head, the man feels the terror and agony of the moment.

What is happening? What have I gotten into now?

Looking down at his leg where the pain entered, he can't see any marks to show where it originated. A metallic clank and scraping catch his attention; he looks up to see two crows have landed on one of the rides in front of him. Watching them, his mind becomes peaceful, at ease.

The voices are closer now; focusing on them, Gerald listens in.

***

One of the 22-year-old souls, Mackenzie Crowley skips ahead of everyone, his black duster dramatically flaring out as he swings his arms out. "Hey man, check out all these crows everywhere! Is this the perfect place, or what?

"Mac, this place is giving me the heebie jeebies." This from the 19-year-old soul, Sheryl Mitchell. "Something's not right here."

"C'mon, Sheryl, this is exactly what we were looking for. We are going to create the first ever Tulane University Steampunk Halloween! Just think, we only have a week, but with this place, everything is already here. It is going to be epic!"

Brian Palmer, the other 22-year-old soul, steps in and tips his bowler cap to Sheryl. "I like it. You should relax, sha." He opens his topcoat, revealing a small .38 revolver. "I'll keep ju safe. My daddy always told me never to go into dark places without preparation."

"Brian, you are such a typical swamper!" The 21-year-old soul, Jared Jones, shakes his head as he kicks a Coca-Cola can into the murk.

"Yeah, well dis here swamper is kicking your ass in Rhetoric Law."

"Ouch." Mackenzie chuckles. "He gotch you dare, Jared."

"Yeah, well, Judge Keminski's an asshole."

"Dat's true; nobody can argue dat." Brian kicks his own can out into the mist, before stopping and looking around. "We are going to have to do some major cleaning up, if we don't want any legal issues of our own."

The four stop, look around and utter a collective moan.

***

Gerald shakes his head in an attempt to block out the voices as he tries to stand up. *I've got to get out of here.* His grip slips off one of the rides, and he tumbles back into the murk, sending the crows to flight. Rolling onto his back, the mental printout continues. *One soul 5 years, one soul lost.*

What the hell is that supposed to mean? He interrupts the mental printout to pry himself up and look around. In the distance, the voices of the students become indiscernible.

To his right, he senses movement near the Joker's Jukebox, one of the few remaining rides that survived the storm. Straining to get upright, and cursing himself for being in this situation, he grabs ahold of the equipment again, but with more determination.

He gains his feet and looks again for any movement. Making his way to the ride, he realizes he is not moving his feet, his legs are barely visible, and he has no clothing on.

Panic sets in and he presses his back against the Joker's Jukebox, hiding himself in the shadows. Looking down at his legs, he watches them ripple and solidify. One of his hands absently touches his chest, and he feels heat coming from the center of it.

Pressing his eyes shut with his other hand, his memories flood to the front of his thoughts--the winds, the heavy rains, trudging through the shoulder high water, the men with guns jumping up out of the water. He winces again as he reflects on what happened.

Three men in wetsuits jump out of the water leveling Glocks towards him. The one on the left, lowers his gun and steps forward. "Gerald, you coward. I knew you couldn't follow through."

Before he can respond, the center man takes off his mask. "Gerald, c'mon sha, you need to do dis."

"Wha ta hell? Hey, doan I know you?" Years of Bayou instincts kick in, as a hint of copper can be smelled in the wind. Gerald looks down at the guy's leg. "D'jou are bleedin'. Ju know you can't be here like dis, doin' dat."

"Ju need to get dat safe! So, we can get otta here an get ourselves a drink."

The leader takes another step, once again pointing his gun at Gerald. "Mr. Malcom, I suggest you listen to your friend--then we all can get a drink. JP wants that safe and you are supposed to get it for him."

"I know wha dat fat Voodoo bastard wants, and he can float his ass in here an get it himself!"

Crows begin to land around him, pulling him from his memories. The metallic scraping of their claws sends a chill down his back. Gerald looks up at the starry night sky, as his memories return to the last time he was here. The sky was very different then.

The day grows dark as the clouds roll in, blocking the sun. Lightning flashes can still be seen as Hurricane Katrina makes a last-ditch effort to continue her destruction.

The leader maintains his gun at shoulder height, taking aim at Gerald. Before he can do anything else, an alligator leaps out of the water, and its jaws clamp down on the waist of the man who was bleeding, pulling him into a death roll and dragging him underwater.

The leader turns and begins to fire at the alligator, as the third man in the party dives into the water in an attempt to swim away. A few feet later, another massive stir develops in the dark water, telling Gerald and the leader that he did not make it.

The leader turns his fire in the direction of the new commotion. Gerald shakes his head, trying to remain motionless. "You ain't gonna do anything wit dat pea-shooter."

The leader spins toward Gerald. "There is one thing I can do."

"Don't . . ."

Gerald's eyes fly open at the sound of an aluminum can hitting one of the rides, and the voices from the nearby souls jar him from his memories. He continues to rub the heated spot on his chest and closes his eyes, remembering the pain.

Struggling and trying to remain as motionless as he can. Feeling the presence of a giant prehistoric beast swimming past him, he hears the leader splashing towards him. He squints his eyes closed as hard as can, and waits for it. As the splashing gets closer, he feels a powerful surge leap from the water, taking down the leader with a howling scream.

Gerald lifts his bleeding shoulder out of the water, feeling the rain as the sky opens up once again. He tries to fight through the pain and drift toward something he can use to pull himself up, knowing if he tries to run he will become another alligator snack. A glint of something in the water catches his attention.

"Wha da hell is dat?" he thinks out loud, before a thought occurs to him. "Perhaps I can salvage this."

Searing pain from the center of his chest interrupts the flood of memories. Struggling not to cry out in pain, he throws his head back, slamming it into the ride. The metallic bang echoes through the park causing murders of crows to take flight.

***

At the metallic echo, Sheryl jumps behind Jared, grabbing his shoulders, and Brian pulls out his revolver with uncanny speed.

Makenzie spins around looking for what caused the noise, his arms out, as if holding it away.

Feeling her grip on his shoulders tighten, Jared whispers loudly, "What was that? Did you guys see anything?"

"We need to get out of here, I knew something was not right with this place."

Gripping the gun with all his might, Brian steps next to Mackenzie. "Dude d'jou see anything?"

"Nah man, but the crows are gone and every hair on my body is standing up right now."

Brian lowers his voice even more, "I know, right? I hate to admit dis, but I think Sheryl is right."

"Don't go all weak on me now." Makenzie looks over his shoulder at Brian, then back at the other two. He is unable to see Sheryl for a moment, until he notices the hands gripping his friend's shoulders. "You two stay here. We're going to look up ahead."

Brian tries not to turn his head, as he looks over at Mackenzie. "Mac, we're gonna do wha?"

Jared doesn't move. "No worries Mac, we ain't debating with you."

Mackenzie looks over at Brian. "Man up. If we're going to use this place, den we have to find out what dat noise was."

"Shit. Let's go."

***

Gerald's ears are ringing, and his mind is flashing lights of pain; yet when he senses movement again, his mind clears instantly, and he turns to face the possible threat.

Watching the crows slowly return, his focus does not waiver as he searches the mist. Out of the shadows, a man's silhouette stands and faces Gerald. It does not make a noise as it slowly drifts towards him.

The moon peeks out from a cloud, and lights up the grotesque facial features of a man who has lived better days.

The man's eyes seem familiar to Gerald, but he can't quite place them. He moves out from the shadows and into the moonlight, to meet this man face to face.

The man remains standing, and he slowly reaches out. His body begins to dissolve, becoming difficult to recognize. His face heals and Gerald recognizes him as one of the three men who ambushed him. The man finishes dissolving into a blur and wisps around Gerald, cutting off any escape route.

Without warning, Gerald's body begins to ripple and absorb the blur. Before Gerald can comprehend what is happening, his mind replays the final moments of the ambush, from this man's memory.

My leg stings. I just want a drink. Let's get this over with. Wait, what was that in the water? What just moved? Teeth! ARRRRGH, so much pain. I can't breathe. I can't see. My lungs burn. I can't breathe.

Gerald lets out an unearthly scream, just as the two boys turn the corner and see him.

"Freeze!" Brian points his gun at Gerald.

Mackenzie looks at him. "Freeze, really? It's a homeless guy! Put the gun down." Removing his black duster, he takes a step toward the man. "Here man, you need dis more than I do right now."

Gerald tilts his head. His eyes widen, realizing again that he doesn't have any clothes on. With one hand covering himself, he quickly reaches out in the direction of the jacket. His hand and forearm transforms to a stream of blurry mist, shooting out of his arm, and scoops the jacket from Mackenzie's hand. The blur returns as Gerald's body absorbs it. He is now wearing the jacket.

Mackenzie and Brian stand in shock, unable to move as they watch the man slowly button the jacket up and wrap the belt around his waist.

Gerald looks up at the two kids as his skin is still solidifying and takes a step toward them. "Thank you."

As if a switch was flipped, the boys turn and run.

Gerald looks down at his hand as it retakes its shape. "So, this is what I have become. Someone (or something), who carries around souls and have to relive their deaths. What did I do to deserve this?"

His thoughts are vocalized, and he can hear them coming from all around him. "What the hell is going on? What has happened to me?"

He senses the crows around him and more fly down and land on the metallic remnants of the adventure ride, their feathery coats shimmering purple in the moonlight. He takes a cautious and weary step back, and swings his arms out to shoo them away. His arms decimate and blurs extend out from the sleeves of the jacket, scattering the crows, but they quickly return to their spots.

One by one the crows tilt their heads towards Gerald. "Looks like I am not getting rid of you guys anytime soon." His chest begins to burn. Without thinking, he massages his sternum and remembers the bone-like artifact with strange writing on it he found in the flood waters.

Pausing, he concentrates on the slightest noises around him--the metallic scraping of the crows' claws, as they shift their weight and take off. Soon, the breeze is the only sound he can hear.

Taking a deep breath, Gerald looks up to the full moon and puts his hands into the coat's pockets.

His right hand discovers something, and he removes it. Taking a look at it, a feeling calm washes over him. "Well, this is a start."

~ ~ ~

Laurel Street, New Orleans, LA
October 25, 2017 - 0035 hours

A tall lanky man leans back on the wooden power pole outside of his small two-bedroom rental. The full moon gleams off of his gold pin-striped vest. Reaching inside it, he pulls out a lighter, and lights his extended pipe, taking a long inhale from it. Holding his breath, feeling the smoke begin to take effect, he hears the squeaking of the wrought iron gate.

"Mac!" Sheryl's stage whisper is loud in the quiet night. "Are you seriously smoking that outside?"

Mackenzie coughs, sputters the breath he was holding, and his top hat goes tumbling into the street. "Keep it down woman. After tonight, I think this is justified."

Jared steps around from behind Sheryl. "Seriously, what did happen? Brian's in there practically catatonic, and the whole trip home, neither one of you gave any disclosure as to what went down."

Taking in an audible inhale and a lengthy exhale, Mackenzie watches his friends intently, as they look to him for answers. Craning his neck to pop it, he starts to light his pipe again.

Sheryl quickly steps in and knocks it from his hand. "Damn it, Mac! What the hell did you see?"

Fury flashes across his brow as the moonlight highlights his bloodshot eyes. He mentally counts to ten. "D'jou two really want to know what we witnessed tonight? I will tell you. If you choose not to believe me, dat's on you; I won't be cross ex'd . . . you got dat?"

Sheryl and Jared give each other a quick glance then both gave him a nod.

"Alright then, the only way to describe what we saw, was . . . Death. Not gory death, but Death itself, struggling with life. We witnessed angels and demons coming together--Paradise Lost meets Dante's Inferno, all of that, in a naked man. A man who now has my coat." Pausing to crack his neck again, he leans down and recovers his pipe. "Now if you will excuse me, I need to exorcise my reality for a few moments."

Jared hooks Sheryl's arm. "Fine, we will see you on Monday. Promise us this, if Brian doesn't come around by morning, you'll get him to the hospital."

Mackenzie gives them an acknowledging lift of his pipe as he watches then get into their car and drive off.

Exhaling the breath he was holding, he hears a voice behind him. "Dat was a poetic description ju gave dare."

Lunging forward as if something punched the back of his knees, Mackenzie recovers his balance and spins around, scanning for the source of the voice.

Recognizing his coat, he notes the strange man is a good six inches shorter than he is, causing the coat to fall flush with the sidewalk. Examining the man, or whatever he is, all Mackenzie can make out is his coat, and a greased-up Saints cap. The brim of the hat is casting a moonlight shadow over the face below it.

Mackenzie slowly steps backward. "Look mister, I doan know you, we dint mean to trespass. We were just looking for a place to have a Halloween party."

Gerald looks at the ground and sees the top hat as the winds shifts its position. He takes his hand out of his pocket and reaches for it. Instead, blurs shoot out of the coat sleeve and scoop up the hat. The blurs carry it over to Mackenzie. "My name is Gerald, and you dropped your hat."

"Ummm . . . th-th-thank you?"

Mackenzie grabs the hat, and the blur immediately returns to the sleeve, causing it to ripple as a hand reforms.

For a moment, neither of them says anything.

Gerald tips his head, looking back at the ground. To Mackenzie, it looks as if the man is listening for something.

Before he can ask anything, two shadowy figures make their way from behind a parked car, the moonlight shimmering off one of their guns. Slurred and barely audible, the gun holder takes the lead. "Turn around slowly, and lemme see da hands."

Gerald lifts his arms slowly to study the expressions on the faces of the assailants. "Look sha, it is not your time. You should both go home."

The second man gives his friend and small push. "Gid a load of dis asshole." He turns his attention back to Mackenzie and Gerald. "He said, get your mofo hands up."

Gerald methodically turns around, straightens his head slightly, and quickly throws his arms out. Blurs immediately reach out toward the two punks. The foggy mist appears to extend through them, and pulls something hard to recognize from both of their bodies.

The assailant's bodies go limp, and drop to the ground.

The streams return to Gerald, as a visible ripple shoots down his back. He shakes his arms, as if he is trying to shake these newly acquired blurs from his hands.

Bringing his hands near his face, he keeps his voice low. "Go home, it is not your time."

The twin streams shoot back out to the bodies on the ground, then return. Gerald's entire body begins to ripple, before solidifying once more.

The assailants look around as if trying to get their bearing. When they recognize the black duster they scramble to their feet. Pure terror is engraved on their faces as they tear off down the street.

Gerald turns back around to face Mackenzie, and hears him exasperate, "Whoa! Holy . . . Wha did . . . How did . . . If you do that again, my friend and I are both gonna need psych evals."

"Yes, well all of dis is new to me too. As for your friend, it is not his time."

"Wat does dat mean? Why are you here? You can keep my jacket, I got two more."

"Na friend, relax. Here . . ." Gerald takes his hand out of his pocket, and tosses a long wallet on the ground in front of Mackenzie. "I need your help."

"Way . . . What?"

Gerald steps closer to Mackenzie. "Stay wit me. I need your help."

"Doan come closer, what can I do?"

Gerald opens the jacket. His chest blurs and begins to extend outward. The fog clears enough to reveal a six-inch cylindrical object. It looks similar to bone or ivory, and on it are some pictographs or maybe ancient writing.

"Wha . . . What is that?"

"Dat's what I need your help wid. I need to take a picture and research it, but as you can tell, I'm in no shape."

"No, no, no. I mean yeah, I can see." Makenzie pauses seeming to weigh all his options, then takes his phone out and snaps a few pictures. Exhaling as if he had been holding his breath for hours, he puts the phone back in his pocket.

"Thank you."

"Nah man, thank you. You just saved my life there, and all I gave you was a jacket."

Before he can ramble on any more, the man in front of him becomes hard to see. His coat-draped body shifts into a larger solid blur, then drifts upward into the cloudless night.

Mackenzie leans down and picks up his wallet, then investigates the packing in his pipe. Trying to settle his nerves, he taps the pipe, emptying the ash onto the street. "Rest, lots of rest; dat's what the doctor ordered."

He walks into the house, and sees Brian standing at the island counter in the kitchen, taking a long drink from a bottle of Bacardi. "Man, wha' da hell was dat, wha' we seen tonight?"

Mackenzie keeps walking to his room, rubbing his arms in an effort to smooth out his permanent goose bumps. "You doan know the half of it."

Missing Robbie
Christopher Buckley

Remember when the universe
was still made up of pulp?
Before in techno we were versed,
when monsters made us gulp?
Back when we still rode rocketships
up to the starry skies—
improbable our whimsy trips,
unlikely to so fly.

We all lived in a Golden Age
of magazines and screen.
Where hero-spacemen were the rage
and rescued the last scene.
Those tentacles and laser beams
and two-way radios,
return a simpler time, it seems,
before we had to grow.
I miss the operatic tropes,
those gizmos and robots.
I miss those times of boyhood hopes
and pseudo-science thought.

I wonder if The Time Machine
could space/time fabric crack.
A reread that could intervene
and somehow send me back...

...back to Amazing Stories days
and flipping through Weird Tales,
returned to sepia sci-fi haze,
in all clichéd detail . .

Hello from the Children of Earth

Curtis A. Deeter

"This is a present from a small, distant world, a token of our sounds, our science, our images, our music, our thoughts, and our feelings. We are attempting to survive our time so we may live into yours."

-President Jimmy Carter

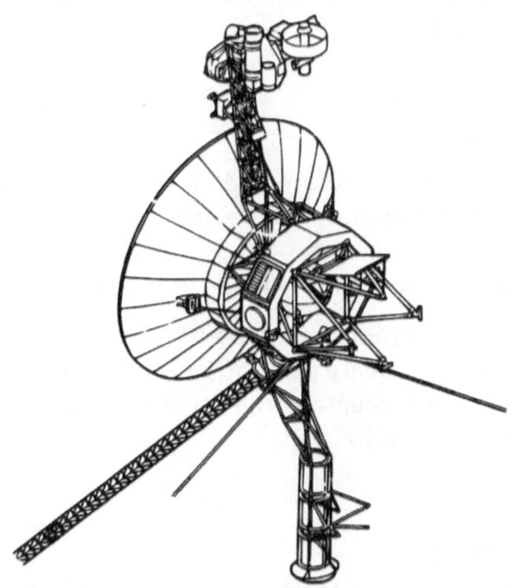

September 5th, 1977.

Voyager 1 launches from Cape Canaveral, Florida, a mere sixteen days after its twin, Voyager 2. They both make their journey into space aboard Titan-Centaur rockets, a propulsion system that the world would never see again. The Voyager 1 leaves Earth's atmosphere with a specific mission in mind: pass by Jupiter, Saturn, and Saturn's largest, atmosphere-thick moon Titan.

March 5th, 1979.

Voyager 1 passes by Jupiter, photographing it and two of its satellite moons, Io and Europa. *Fact: Io was named for one of Zeus's lovers, a Priestess of the Goddess Hera.* It was either Zeus—as a means to hide his mortal lover from Hera—or Hera herself, who turned Io into a heifer. As a mistress of science, and a mountain-spotted world, the name Io is indeed suitable.

Fact: Europa is considered one of the best options for future habitability. With an ice-crust and a thin, oxygen-rich atmosphere, science-fiction and science-reality alike, look to places like these with hope and adoration.

November 12th, 1980.

Voyager 1 passes by Saturn and photographs a kink in one of its outer rings. Consisting mostly of ice and rock of infinitesimal size and composition, the F ring seems to have hit a bump in the road, so to speak. Speculation says Saturn's moon Prometheus is to blame.

A long time ago, Prometheus stole fire from the gods. Now, it seems Prometheus is out to steal a piece of Saturn. The jury is still out on how Prometheus's smaller counterpart, Pandora, feels about all of this. It's a box no one is prepared to open.

February 14th, 1990.

As Voyager 1 approaches the threshold between the Milky Way and interstellar space, it takes a snapshot of the Solar System as seen from outside.

This "family portrait', taken at a distance of 6 billion kilometers from Earth, is a mosaic of 60 individual frames. It's underwhelming at first glance, but imagine getting 100 billion family members together in one place at one time, and then making sure Auntie Sue keeps a straight face and the twins stop moving about around the edges of the shot.

February 17th, 1998.

Voyager 1 passes Pioneer 10, becoming the farthest man made object in space, as it approaches the edge of the solar system. Champagne and congratulatory high-fives all around.

Carl Sagan's vision of "advanced space-faring civilizations in interstellar space" is one step closer to becoming a reality. Sadly, after a two year struggle with myelodysplasia—a disease in which blood cells within the bone marrow do not mature into healthy, viable cells—he passed just a year or so before he could witness this expansion of the known universe.

August 25th, 2012.

Voyager 1 officially crosses the heliopause, a bubble of plasma blowout from the Sun that separates the Milky Way and the interstellar medium. The echoes of the deaths of millions of stars are the spacecraft's only friends now.

In an ironic and tragic turn of events, just as we make yet another "giant leap for mankind", Neil Armstrong dies after heart surgery.

January 2nd, 2020.

Voyager 1 begins its own inevitable death. Gyroscopic operations terminate. The bus begins to shut down, causing the electronics within the shuttle to flicker and die one by one like the stars they were created to observe. The cameras no longer operate. Even if they did, the optical calibration system wouldn't be able to guide their viewfinders. The ultraviolet spectrometer clicks off after a brief stint of reanimation, but that's okay. From here, there's just the Oort cloud and 40,000 years of oblivion.

June 20th, 2025.

A blink of the eye before Voyager 1 shuts all of its systems down forever, something amazing happens.

A camera inside the space shuttle, dark for over five years, fizzles to life. First, static dances across the screen in streaks of gray like ants racing home to their queen. Then, the rows widen and contract. Finally, the fisheye picture comes to life.

No one's watching at first. Why would they be? NASA's budget has been slashed to nothing, while privateers streak across the sky in luxury space yachts. The government spends what little money is left cleaning up the environmental fallout. Why would they waste even a penny on someone to watch a blank screen?

The janitor, Suzy Stone, happens by in yet another cosmic coincidence. It's her first month on the job, and she's not sure what she's looking at. Dust settles over the furniture in the Jet Propulsion Laboratory—a nondescript office building in Pasadena—despite the impending shut down of one of the world's most ambitious scientific ventures, and somebody has to keep things tidy. The last guy retired after almost 40 years, and even with triple the time under her belt, Suzy is sure she wouldn't be able to comprehend the sudden, startling images.

After a quick phone call, a team of scientists, graduate students, and random passersby, some still in their robes and others intoxicated from Friday night shenanigans, huddle around a single computer monitor. Their mouths are gaping and their eyes are wide. No one says a word. No one as much as sneezes for hours.

No one believes what they are seeing.

The thing—whatever it is—is not gray with an elongated conical head, nor is it tiny and green with suckers on its fingertips. It doesn't have tentacles growing out of the back of its skull, or horns protruding from its temples. In fact, it's impossible to say what it *does* have. It's a semi-humanoid blur; a blip in the light, stretching from catwalk to ceiling. The interior of the shuttle shifts and warps as it rifles around, pulling wires out and removing sheets of metal from the wall as if it were peeling an onion.

Then, it speaks.

It shouldn't be able to speak, and they shouldn't be able to hear it. The words start out garbled. At first, the aural curiosities are alien and dissonant.

The audience cringes and cups their hands over their ears. After several hours, the sounds become almost harmonic and are belted out in rhythmic bursts.

"Hey, I know this jam," Suzy Stone says. It's the first time anyone has said anything for almost 18 hours, and her riveted companions recognize it too. They're all humming "Johnny B. Goode" together, but not loudly enough to outshine the heavenly soundwaves pouring out of the monitor. The words of Chuck Berry make the surreal video feed seem normal.

Almost.

The being is ever so slightly more defined, as if the 50's vibes have the congenital ability to bring tangible substance to ethereal and formless things. As it becomes clearer, it's unmistakable—this extraterrestrial anomaly is dancing to the tunes.

"Anyone wanna order pizza?" somebody suggests, to a response of *uh huh's* and *ehh's*.

The delivery driver arrives two hours later, with thirty pizzas.

Nobody bothers to tip, but she doesn't head back to the shop either. She can't miss even a second of what's unfolding on the screen.

After a long spurt of silence the audience is anxious. They shuffle awkwardly. They grind their teeth. They smoke cigarettes down to their wet filters.

All the while, the alien is hunched over a viewscreen of its own, within Voyager 1. It's now got extremities, which it uses to swipe from one side to the other in front of the screen without ever touching the glass. Faint and distorted images appear and disappear with each flick of its wrist.

Two big, unspoken questions loom over the audience like a supernova. *They didn't have touch screens in the seventies, did they?* And *is it just me, or is that thing becoming more... human?*

What they didn't ask is *how will this creature perceive humanity, once it's seen what we're capable of?*

When it leaves the monitor, it has skin, and joints, and hair. It turns to the camera slowly, deliberately, and the pizza delivery driver passes out. From snapshots it has seen from Earth—116 images chosen by the original Voyager 1 scientists—it's morphed itself into a monstrous, patchwork of what it must think humans look like.

Its skin is all wrong, patchy and discolored and overlapping in places. Across its face the skin is stretched too taught. On its arms it hangs loose and dry. One pectoral muscle clings to the outside of its chest, and what appears to be an umbilical cord dangles from its abdomen. It's part man, part woman, and part animal, with young eyes and an ancient, disfigured smile. A series of silver fish fins protrude from its spine.

It reaches a striped, taloned hand towards the camera lens and taps three times. The room in Pasadena shakes. A coffee cup falls off the desk and spills day-old coffee all over the surge protector. The power spikes and the lights go off, but the monitor stays on.

With one grotesque eyeball pressed up against the lens, the alien says in broken English, "Hello Children of Earth."

Then, "Bonjour tout le monde. Chân thành gửi tới các bạn lời chào thân hữu. Witajcie, istoty z zaświatów. Желимо вам све најлепше са наше планете," etcetera, etcetera.

Most of these sounds—greetings from 55 different languages—sound foreign and harsh to the audience. The alien grows more and more animated as it seamlessly transitions from one linguistic family to another, as if playing back a recording. The worst part comes at the end, in the form of bellowing whale sounds and life-like dolphin trills.

Suddenly, the stream of acoustic consciousness ends. The alien backs away from the camera, the wetness of its eye leaving a slimy streak across the feed, and bows one way and then to the other, as if thanking the audience for its time and admiration. It reaches its other hand—this one possessing long, slender fingers with protrusile suckers—towards the camera inside of Voyager 1, and sends it through the screen.

It comes out the other side and suctions to Suzy Stone's forehead, then yanks violently. Her face smacks into the computer monitor and blood pours from her nose. Then it tosses her from one side to the other, banging her into the floor over and over, before discarding her wildly into the crowd.

Everyone begins screaming and bumping into each other trying to escape, but it's too late; the alien is grasping the edges of the monitor with talons and suckers. It's pulling itself out of the interior of Voyager 1, and into the Southern California lab. Four times taller than even the biggest human present, it dances from one victim to another singing its song of death.

June 21st, 2025.

A local detective watches the CCTV feed of the previous day's horror. He doesn't believe his own eyes. He can't. He hadn't believed the delivery driver's story—who'd survived only because she'd been passed out when the alien came through—either.

No sane man would.

The surgical precision with which the alien slaughtered the people in that room, as if it had been handed the anatomical blueprints of humanity and a choreographed play-by-play of human nature, startles the detective. He's not by any means squeamish, but he vomits on his loafers by the second act. At intermission, he's on the floor, retching and sobbing.

No one else has seen the alien of course, but the sounds of Chuck Berry continue to ceaselessly emanate from the powerless monitor in the evidence room. Four people from IT have been through to try and shut it down. Four people from IT have failed to do so.

He fast-forwards through the more gruesome parts of the footage. One can only stomach so much carnage, so many rolling heads, before losing the will to go on. He pauses it at the same moment the alien discovers the camera. The creature is staring right at him as if it knows he's watching.

Without hitting play, the alien moves in jerking stop-motion. It steps over the corpses towards the camera and reaches towards the detective. A powerful hand extends through the lens like it is water, and grabs him by his tie.

Voyager 1 shuts down, forever destined to float alone through the void of space.

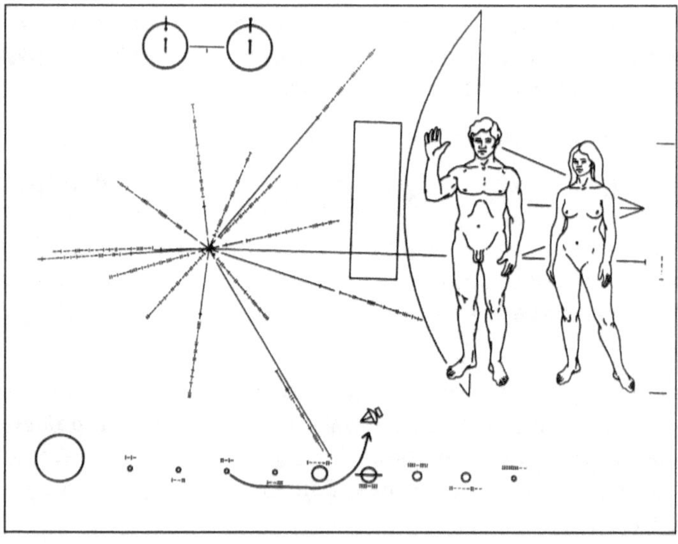

Utopia In Space
John Grey

Ah such splendor, such grandeur,
the splendor of ancient civilizations
recreated on a distant planet
down to the last stone,
the last marble god.

Ideals are unafraid
of desolate landscapes.
Art and knowledge
stand up to threatening air.
The barrenness in outer space
is ripe tor grand design
Utopia on Caerius 4?
Why not?

Brave facades
take no lip from hostile nature.
Esthetics root down
in lifeless soil.
A quest for beauty
embraces the
ugliness around.

Here is Rome,
here is Athens,
here is Alexandria,
peopled by pioneer artists,
spacemen philosophers,
the wise and the strong,
the gallant and the great.

But the devil is in the mountain,
his fire cannot be denied,
one clamoring burst
and flame and larva
rain down on dreams,
raze ambition.
turn majesty to ash.

Utopia on Careius 4?
At least until the wind blows.

Pen Pal

Wim Verveen

A nagging sound in the distance is disturbing the idyllic feeling of my wonderful semi-awake state. No. The land of dreams is too tempting. I need more rest and drift some with the clouds. Leave me alone. The voice grew in importance, ignoring my pleas and silencing a lovely dream. The voice became more metallic and was now traceable to the alarm clock next to my bed.

"Good morning, get up please."

"Good morning, get up please. This a warning."

The damn thing clearly didn't want to shut up. Vaguely aware of it's presence, I waved at it in the faint hope it might indeed mind its own business from now on.

"Notice: One point will be subtracted from your social credit in 5 - 4 - 3 - 2 . . ."

I was upright and out of my bed in a mere fraction of a second, sending the sheets hurling away as violently as an exploding grenade, in response to this threat.

"Good morning Eveline, and have a nice day. Remember, getting up on time is good for your health. You currently have one hundred points. Please read your daily review on tips to do better."

"And a bloody good day to you as well."

My head hurt from smashing against the floor when I tripped over my shoes, but the stupid clock wasn't intimidated by my murderous looks. Violence was no option anyway, I didn't even want to know how many credits that would be.

I jumped up and hit the shower. Liwei was already up, hopefully making coffee. Gasping, I let the water freeze my skin; totally not to my liking.

"Hotter."

"Warning. Cold water is healthier. Ten points for more heat."

"Ah damn it! Do it. Ah . . . that's lovely."

When I finally entered the living room after wasting another credit on a few extra minutes, Liwei had already finished his breakfast, consisting of yogurt, dried fruit and grains. The fridge was void of the necessities of life like eggs, sausages, and of course, bacon. Regulations apparently. I work out all the time, there is really no logic why I can't have it.

The smell of freshly fried bacon begins to rise up from my memories--an olfactory reminder of home, and the day the message arrived on my timeline.

***

Hi, I'm Liwei. Please accept my request.

How many of such messages do I get a day? At least three; there was no way I was going to react this time.

Then I noticed his face, the color in his eyes.

I had to know more about this character popping up on my time-line. I clicked accept before I became consciously aware of what I did. His status changed to friend. A wave on my messenger. Taking a deep breath I began to type, no harm really, I could stop at any time I wanted.

The first few weeks, nothing much happened. We chatted now and then--whenever our time zones collided in the proper rhythm.

Without warning, that all changed.

One day when he wasn't there during the weekend, I noticed I missed his presence. I kept staring at my phone the entire weekend in hopes of some sort of response, but nothing happened.

When he finally resurfaced on Tuesday, I was thrilled and worried at the same time.

He explained he had been out of credits.

I wondered if it really was the money; maybe it was just a ploy to have me wire some. For a second I thought he was just like all the others, but then he didn't mention it again, and we returned to our normal routine.

Liwei wasn't like any of the others at all. No indecent proposals from the get go, but someone who was intelligent and humorous. He gladly talked about his country, as long as it didn't involve politics. He really hated to talk about that.

Understandable.

"You look tired Eveline."

"Sorry Liwei, tough day at work."

"Oh, I'm sorry. Watch my smile and imagine we're holding hands."

I smiled back and already felt better.

Our relation intensified. We swapped pictures and had video chats with increasing frequency. His country looked so nice, much better than I envisioned.

"It's the new policies on health and environment," he said and explained how much worse it used to be before the current government implemented a major change.

I began to long to go.

As he spoke I watched his lips. Time slowed down when it happened... my finger traced his face on the screen. I could feel how we touched, but then we didn't and it saddened me. I wanted more; I wanted to meet this guy, with his witty humor and smiling face. I wanted to smell his scent and let my fingers move through his hair. I wanted to be in his arms.

"You mean I can just go over there? No restrictions?"

"Not at all. Our government encourages people like you to come. In fact, we make sure you get settled in our social benefit system and enjoy the time you spend; maybe you will even stay. You have a referral already."

"Referral?"

"Oh I'm sorry. I didn't explain. Our government encourages people to engage with each other, and if so credits them in our system. We want happy--and above all healthy--people. Thank you so much for being part of it."

I noticed a number on the display of his bracelet increasing when he spoke to me.

I thought it was some sort of company customer-centric program, like those springing up all over the place recently. Yes, that must be it; immediate gratification is a powerful tool for influencing behavior. He helped me get my visa, with an unlimited stay. Wow.

***

Then came the first moment in the airport, after touching down on foreign soil. The line in front of customs, and the weary feeling this might not be true, that I might be sent back.

Why would they let someone like me fly here and enter their country with no restrictions?

Further in the distance I saw a glass wall, and behind it, people watching. This was different from most airports. Frantically, I searched for his face.

"Can you come with me miss?"

Something went wrong; the visa must be invalid. I knew it--no limit... it had all sounded too good to be true.

The floor below me liquefied, and I began to sink. What if it wasn't my visa? Where was my luggage? Had they kept it for further examination? A drug dealer could have slipped contraband in it.

Oh my god! I'm screwed. They are going to lock me away forever. This is the end.

Like a lamb to the slaughter, I followed him to an office, and I felt the cold steel of a cuff on my wrist.

"It's my honor to provide you your own complementary Health & Happiness bracelet. The government, and the Department of Health & Happiness, wish you a pleasant stay. To this end, we have provided you with a token amount of credits, to help you settle in."

The bracelet came alive as soon as it touched my skin. I watched the number on his bracelet increase as he talked to me.

My phone buzzed, and showed that it was connected to my bracelet as well. The display notified me that I had been given six thousand credits, sixty times the number on the bracelet of the official.

He saw me eye him and smiled. "Hospitality is considered a virtue in this land. We welcome people, especially ladies. Please feel at home."

Another tick on his bracelet.

Slightly puzzled I walked toward the exit. his words still lingering in my brain.

The doors opened, and behind them, he stood waiting.

Liwei.

My thoughts were extinguished instantly, and I was mesmerized by his appearance. His arms around me moments later, our lips meeting for the first time. All the times I had traced those lips with my fingers. All the times I had dreamed of touching him...

***

"You should have breakfast. It's a health regulation."

I smiled at Liwei. Of course, I should. It's sound advice.

I gazed at my bracelet. What a stupid system, eat healthy and get points. Want hot water? Pay with credits. It's my decision to eat or not.

Alas, that smile on his face. I can't say no to that.

I filled my plate with the required food and began to eat; the tick on my bracelet felt oddly like a reward. We touched hands as we continued to eat. My bracelet ticked again, the moment we made contact. Quite a bit of technology, if it can register such details.

I watched the central counter in the home. Over ten thousand--our combined amount. I had transferred almost all my credits for safe-keeping last night. He had told me it would make sure they wouldn't be lost if my bracelet was stolen. It seemed like a good suggestion at the time.

Apparently, he received the same amount as I did just for getting me here. Weird, really. I was curious, but waited until Liwei kissed me and went to work.

Attend to the dishes? Sure, why not.

***

"Call Mother."

"You do not have enough credits."

What?

Oh damn! I had transferred so much, that after the shower only a little was left. How did I get the rest out of that central counter? It didn't matter how much I tried.

Apparently, I needed his fingerprint to access my funds. How inconvenient; this was clearly something we needed to change. Luckily I could at least browse around the internet, look up this happiness program.

"One credit for over extensive internet use."

This bracelet was going to get on my nerves. I was at his place all day, Why should it care that I'm surfing the web? Strangely enough I couldn't find much on the program; my fist was beginning to crush the mouse in frustration.

I had an idea. Maybe I should go out and find a library or ask the right people to discover how it works.

"Two credits for over extensive internet use."

Silently cursing the damned bracelet, I shut down the computer. I readied myself to leave, and headed for the door.

"Warning, the house is not cleaned."

What am I? The cleaning lady?

The door slammed shut behind me with brute force, and I bit my tongue to keep a curse from flying out of my mouth. I felt the bracelet buzz as it ticked off another credit. This happiness program was really failing at doing what it was intended for.

The next challenge was getting to the library. Taking a cab cost too many credits. Really, Liwei should have told me how expensive some services were, when I transferred my credits to him to keep safe.

I finally managed to get onto a bus. It was wonderfully clean, I must say, but not as fast as I wanted to go.

Slowly it meandered through the city. Luckily, the bracelet kept track of my route, so I didn't need to keep an eye out for the right stop. Finally I was able to exit the vehicle, and discovered to my joy it had dropped me in front of the building I had aimed for.

"Happiness & Healthy program? Of course, I want to help you, Miss. It's right over there in the back. Everything you need to know."

Flipping through pages of glossy information didn't tell me much about what the program actually was. I saw many smiling faces--small kids playing in playgrounds, and happy couples frolicking in meadows. It did tell me the program was started by the current president, some twenty years ago, before they lifted the term limits. Apparently he was immensely popular, according to an old article, published right before the last election.

My vision trained on some small print below the article.

Come and vote for our president and you will receive one hundred credits donated by our major industries.

That's odd.

I sent a message to one of my friends back home, to inquire if they could find out anything about it. One more credit gone.

"Can I help you, Miss?"

A uniformed man had appeared. He was well groomed and his clothing had clearly been ironed by a master at the art. There were symbols on his clothes which I recognized as belonging to the Department of Happiness & Health. He waited quietly for my response.

"I'm just learning about the Happiness & Health program."

"A wonderful initiative which should be applauded. However, paper information can be so dull. I would be happy to provide you with anything you need. Reading old election data of our great president isn't really leading you anywhere."

I had no idea how he knew I was reading this from the point where he was standing, until I realized I had just sent an email about the exact same subject.

My phone buzzed eerily at that same moment. I looked at the screen and discovered my email was returned. "Illegal citizen action," it noted. My bracelet ticked down five credits.

"I'm just trying to learn, mister."

"It's Inspector, and there is really not much to know. The Ministry of Happiness & Health works hard every day to make sure all citizens are happy and healthy, by encouraging them to do the right thing."

"How do I know what the right thing is?"

"You don't need to. Your bracelet is connected to our vast computer systems, and will guide you by giving you credits when you perform properly to standards."

"Who determines those standards?"

"It's highly inappropriate to criticize the President, Miss. I think it's best you take care of other citizen duties, such as making your bed. Good day."

Gasping I watched him leave.

These guys know everything!

I needed to talk to Liwei as soon as he got home.

Hurriedly I left the library, just in time to see the bus leave. No matter, it gave me some time discover the city; since my arrival, Liwei and I had spent most of our time in his place, too occupied to go out and explore.

The city was vast. Skyscrapers towering above the other buildings, one of them being where Liwei lived.

Where we lived.

Only a few cars were about, all of them driven automatically like the buses, yet the roads told a story of another time, where this wasn't the case.

I noticed a gym, with free access for all citizens. Inside I found all the usual equipment, but all every piece had a screen tied to the bracelet of the user. Slowly their counters went up as they performed their exercises.

I left the place and checked out a supermarket. There were no cash registers anywhere; everything was deducted from the balance on your bracelet. Sadly, there was nothing I could buy, with the small amount I carried. The entertainment section was rather sparse and seemed to consist mostly of educational content.

A figure wearing a long coat approached me.

"Interested in more entertainment than offered here?"

"What do you mean?"

"Movies, the real ones not the ones which make it through the Health & Safety board."

He opened his coat, and I could see a number of movies attached to the inside, all priced in hard currency. I remembered I had left my credit card at home. I shook my head and the guy disappeared into the shop.

Minutes later, a uniformed man appeared--the same one I had met in the library.

"I see you're interested in entertainment. I would advise you to stick to the local offerings."

Leaving the shop, I noticed a black van outside. The guy with the movies was visible inside, and just before the door closed, he yelled something at me.

"They're watching."

Uneasily, I took the bus home. When I arrived at the apartment, Liwei was already there.

His smell was awesome.

***

Hours later, I finally got up and grabbed his shirt to wear, and returned to the living room.

The first thing I noticed was the central counter. The number was down, three thousand to be precise.

"Liwei, what happened to all those health credits?"

"No worries honey."

His lips were so soft. His arms so strong. My mind drifted away on the waves of attention he gave me. Curled against each other, we watched some educational television, our fingers intertwining. All thoughts about the guy in the library faded. How could I be possibly be happier than I was now?

***

"Can you clean the house while I'm at work?"

I said yes before I even realized I said it.

Soon, I found myself vacuuming the rooms one by one. At least I could be somewhat useful until I found a real job. The radio played in the background, mostly unfamiliar music.

My language courses paid off as I was listening to the words. After a while I began to keep up the pace, until the music was interrupted by the news. Curious on the local happenings I listened.

"The new policies of the government to restore gender balance have been successful. Citizens are encouraged to participate. Free internet access for all male citizens younger than thirty."

The hose fell on the floor and the sound died away as I headed for the computer.

What kind of program was this? What was going on?

I pulled up a search page on the subject, and the screen unexpectedly went blank.

Out of credits.

I grabbed my coat and was almost out the door, when I realized I had forgotten my credit card again.

Quickly I returned and rummaged through my stuff, but my card was nowhere to be found, nor was the paper money I was sure I had brought with me.

Ignoring this fact, I headed out again and didn't have to go far before hearing another ad, intended for young men.

By the time I reached the library, my feet were killing me. This time the lady behind the counter eyed me differently, and as I began to walk away, the same uniformed officer from yesterday barred my progress.

"I want to go in."

"Your credit is zero, Miss. You shouldn't be in the library, but performing your civic duties."

"I'm a tourist."

"Oh are you? According to my sources, you've received a migration visa."

"Wait… What? That isn't true. Look, this only says I can stay indefinitely."

"A new request has been made by your husband, Miss."

"What?! That can't be true, I'm not…"

"You need to return home, Miss. There is housework to be done."

My hands cramped as I ran out into the street.

This was insane! Not only the way the officer had spoken to me, but the things he knew. Apart from that, there was the stunt (*my husband*) Liwei had pulled as well. We were going to have a really strong discussion about this.

I grabbed my phone and attempted to uninstall the Happiness & Health app. *Not allowed.* Annoyed, I turned the device off.

"Warning. Health & Safety regulation breach. Please turn your phone back on."

I folded my hands and rested against the wall.

What if I don't do it?

The screen of the bracelet changed to red, and it began to repeat its warning. I stared at the sky, until the sound of an approaching car drew my attention.

A car with blue stripes parked next to me, and two dark clad men stepped out. "Please join us miss."

I didn't want to go, but they were quite insistent and guided me to the back of the car. They didn't say a word during the trip. They took me to a police building, where I was guided to a small room, with a table and two chairs on each side. They sat me in one, and took up positions across from me.

No matter what I said, or how hard I tried to draw their attention, they remained silent. Finally the door opened, and Liwei entered, his face worried. He sat down next to me.

One of the men then started to talk.

"I'm glad you're here. Your wife has been apprehended for attempting to evade lawful monitoring."

"Wait I'm not his…"

The quieter of the two men raised his hand in a gesture that obviously meant I needed to shut up. The other continued to talk to Liwei in a rather up-tempo manner, with Liwei apologizing regularly.

We didn't speak in the car all the way back to his apartment. Once we were inside, we did--and we had our first fight.

"You need to stop doing what you're doing and pay attention to your civic duties."

"I can go wherever I want! I'm a free person."

"Of course you are, but until you do as I say, I'm not giving you any more credits. Next time we could be fined for your behavior!"

"My behavior?! They grabbed me from the street. I expected you to be more supportive. I flew half the world to be here. You're not telling me what to do!"

"Yes, I am. Now go finish the housework or I'll call them myself."

I was flabbergasted. Tears welled up as I rushed to the bedroom and slammed the door. I must have fallen asleep while crying.

When I finally returned to the living room Liwei was sitting down, as if nothing had happened. The vacuum cleaner was still where I had left it. Not a word was spoken.

The next day, I fired up the computer. I had to know where the embassy was. There was no connection. *Out of credits.* Angrily, I slammed my fist on the table.

An idea formed in my head.

I began to dutifully clean the house. Lo and behold, one by one credits appeared. A lunch with just some fruit added even more. When I had finished all I could do, I had gathered a significant amount.

This time, I finally made it to the world wide web, and could look up the embassy's address. It was located in a special district, far away from the part of the city where I was.

I grabbed my phone and checked the route. *Not Accessible.* I keyed in the phone number and tried it that way. "Not accessible," a machine voice said. I felt really cold. I tried to send an email to my parents, but again it gave the same message.

The link at the bottom of the message screen drew my attention. In search of an explanation, I clicked it, and waited patiently for it to load.

The Ministry of Health & Happiness.

"Credit too low, due to social misbehavior." There were also some explanations, but they didn't seem to make sense.

Restricted travel for socially under adapted civilians?

My face warmed up to the point that sweat formed on my brow. I sat behind the screen for a long while, then stood.

I had to do something.

***

The next few days I was excruciatingly nice and polite to Liwei. I cooked dinner every day, cleaned the house and washed his clothes. He didn't say thank you once, and behaved as if I had done this for years. Slowly I grew irritated about his behavior, but didn't say a word.

My credit level began to rise, slowly but steadily. I upped the ante, by washing the windows and cleaning the closets. That's when I noticed the broken power socket.

Guessing Liwei wouldn't mind a wife with some extra skills, I unscrewed the socket in order to replace it, and found opening much larger than needed behind it.

Whistling, I removed several items from this hiding place: a card with a Department of Health & Happiness logo;. a bunch of movies, just like the guy in the store had offered me; a thick wad of dollars; and my credit card and passport.

Finally.

When I recovered my passport, I noticed a letter hidden below it. Curious, I opened it and scanned its contents. The letter was addressed to Liwei.

I gasped when I read it

Conformation of full citizenship for his wife, me. The nerve that this man had! How could I've fallen for this? I had to leave this place immediately.

With all the money I now had access to, I no longer needed the embassy; I could get myself a ticket and fly home. I fired up the internet again, and found one flight that was going back, today.

I had to hurry, in just a few hours it would be gone. No fiber in my body wanted to spend any more time in this place.

I grabbed a few clothes--no more than I could carry in a single bag--and rushed to the door.

It was locked.

That asshole locked me in the house!

I was not going to let that stop me. Cleaning the house had its advantages. I dragged the tool chest I had spotted the other day to the door, and went to work.

"Warning. Socially unacceptable behavior spotted."

"Fuck off, stupid bracelet."

To my surprise it kept quiet. The door quickly succumbed to my violent attempts, and opened. When I went outside, a few people gazed at me strangely. I smiled and hurried away.

The credit balance on the bracelet had gone down significantly, but I didn't care. What I had was enough to get me on the bus to the airport. The doors closed and the vehicle began driving.

My gaze shifted to the house. I ducked. Walking along the curb was that same uniformed civil servant from the library.

How did he get here so fast?

We passed and I looked back. He hadn't noticed me! I sank back onto the seat and relaxed; I had gotten away.

The bus drove through the streets until it reached central station. I disappeared into the crowd and followed the stairs down to the subway.

Nervously I observed people watching me, but they were just curious; there weren't many foreigners like me.

After a while people began minding their own business. The train meandered through the tubes on its way to the airport, where it slowed down. The doors opened and people spilled out on the platform.

When I reached the top of the stairs I could hear the sounds of a plane taking off. It was like music to my ears, but I wasn't safe yet.

Putting on a straight face I retrieved my ticked and proceeded to-wards the security check. Breathing as normally as I could, I watched my bag disappear into the scanner.

A buzzer sounded.

"Miss?"

Oh no, they were on to me! I started to panic. Could I make a run for it? No, these people had guns. Someone began to pat me down, then she smiled and lifted her thumb. It was nothing, false alarm. I sat down with a cup of tea and waited for the gate to open. Several guards passed but none was even remotely interested.

A little voice began to rejoice in my head.

Don't be to happy yet, wait until your in the plane.

The minutes crept forward. Finally. I walked over to the gate.

The plane stood waiting. The last few steps.

I'm safe, I'm finally safe.

The cushion of the seat resting against my back, I closed my eyes. It was only a matter of time now, and I would be out of this hell.

"Miss?"

I knew that voice. No, that couldn't be! It was him. "On behalf of the government, I'm arresting you for gravely breaking the social standards, as laid down by the Department of Happiness & Health."

"No! Go away."

I tried to hit him, but several security guards rushed in. They dragged me, kicking and screaming, away from the plane and towards a waiting car. Cuffs were put on my wrists. Pressed between two large officers the car began to drive, all the way back to the station.

***

"Ah there you are. They haven't allowed me to see you since last week."

I raised myself from the bed and observed Liwei standing on the other side of the bars. An officer opened the door and let me out.

"Come, we need to go home. There is much to do, it has become quite a mess since you left."

Someone put a bracelet on my wrist, and helped me change from the prison uniform to my regular clothes. I looked at the bracelet. The number on it was minus one thousand.

With my head down I followed Liwei outside.

Was I ever going to leave this place?

The Silent Totality

Richard King Perkins II

Atlas shrugged—

and nobody noticed.
No one remembers exactly when
but one day
the world went out—
not with a bang
nor even a whimper.
It ended with a single dispassionate

—yawn.

The Longest Goodbye
Dusty Grein

I always knew this might be a one way trip, but I never thought it would be because there was no home to return to.

Dr. Dalton was a genius. That much was a given. His work on theoretical quantum physics and string theory had been hailed as revolutionary, and many in academic circles had been calling him the new Einstein. I'm pretty sure if things hadn't gone so wrong, he would have been in line to occupy the chair that both Newton and Hawking had occupied.

There are so few of us left now.

I like to think Dr. Dalton was happy that day, sitting with his wife and fellow scientists . . . if only we had known how terribly wrong the reaction would go.

The media had covered the opening celebration of his fusion reactor with all the pomp and circumstance it deserved. At last we would have clean, unlimited energy.

Even here, aboard the space-station, we had stopped our experiments to watch them throw the switch.

It happened quickly.

That was the only consolation there was, for those who had been on the Earth. One minute they were there, having an ordinary day-—the next they were gone, as the entire planet and its atmosphere erupted into a new miniature sun.

We were hurled into deep space, out of the planetary elliptical, by the force of the explosion. Riding the shock wave of energy that almost killed us all with the G-forces of sudden acceleration, we were soon moving at incredible speed.

Based on the view of the stars we can see, including the faint binary we are calling Earth-Sol, we are traveling at about 60% of light speed.

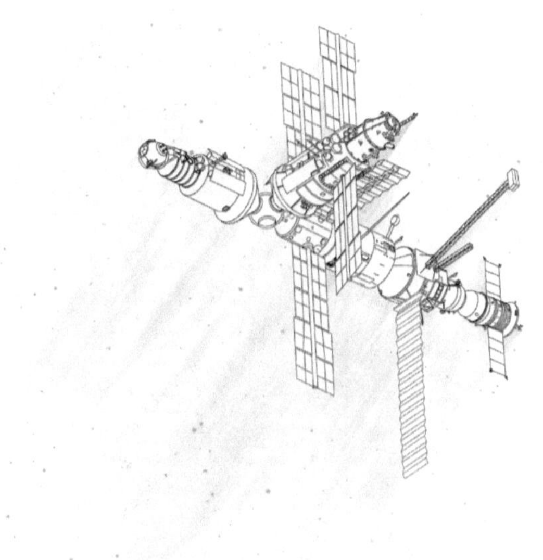

I guess that makes us the fastest humans in history.

Sadly, we are also the last seven representatives of the human race from Earth.

I hope that the air runs out before the heat fails. I think I would rather die that way.

Maybe someday, some other race will find us. Frozen and floating in space, there's a chance our DNA might be used to give our species another shot.

I wonder if my frozen tears will still be on my face.

Senora's Symphony
Alex Collazo

**OPRESSA MAL
SUR SYSTEM,
BLUE OCEAN GALAXY,
20:00 Hours**

Senora crossed the large river, and arrived at the embankment by traveling underwater. She was encased in what the clan called *The Leopards eye*. This special fluorescent bubble was created by swallowing a mixed solvent, then using the power of her spirit energy, *Ke Dekre [The Essence],* to maintain the shape of the sphere which now carried her toward her objective. As she traveled, she stood upright inside the bubble, floating with her eyes closed, her right fist dug into her left open palm.

Two soldiers passed by making their rounds, and missed the translucent globule rise from the water and dissolve as it made contact with dirt and gravel, revealing the beautiful assassin inside. Senora took a few steps, then stopped momentarily to scan the entire area. She tied her wavy auburn hair into a quick ponytail, adjusted her body armor, and pulled her arm guards tight, before making sure her headband was properly fastened.

She walked towards the yellow electrical shield, and once there she closed her eyes and began to meditate. With her eyes still closed, she raised her gloved hands and touched the energy shield.

This shield was designed to kill anyone or anything that dared to touch it, turning them into fragments and pieces of burning meat.

The designers however, had not counted on Senora, who was no mere human--she had been born within the outposts of the MINIAN Clans, and trained since she was a child to eliminate anyone who stood against the forces of truth and justice.

She absorbed the full measure of its power, and the shield deactivated, even as the alarms sounded.

Senora looked up, and for the first time, she saw it in real life--the infamous yet nigh impregnable *Star Fortress of Raahn Sao.*

This stronghold was the home of the vile and immoral dictator, Goth Manusa, who ruled the entire planet of *Opressa Mal* with an iron fist.

Days before, the Tiehrran planetary government had concluded deliberations with Goth and was now at the stage where President Farrs had moved in to take down the Fifth Army of *Opressa,* in hopes to end the torture and suffering the Opressans were undergoing, slavery and death being one of the norms and everyday occurrences under this evil man and would be king.

When the President called on the Minian Shinora clan to assassinate the leaders and mad men in charge of the malignant organization he had said it was to end the subjugation and abuse of the people, once and for all. Senora couldn't resist.

Mame Hunt, The Head and Soveranus of the MINIAN sent Manalex Hunt, his son, to accompany her. "Take a ship to the Planet of *Opressa Mal* and engage in the liberation of the people of that besieged planet. Free the slaves and return them to their normal lives. This is their fresh start at Freedom!" The message still played in Senora's mind as she sprinted toward the Citadel.

She focused her energy and controlled her breathing and muscle contractions. The edifice was a mile and a half away from where she stood and she wanted to engage the enemy as quick as possible. She didn't intend for this mission to ruin her perfect accuracy rating. She ran with supernatural speed.

The wide asphalt road surface was built to sustain large vehicles and planetary ships, for the delivery of slaves no less,but it trembled under the force of her speed and power.

Jungle lined the road to the citadel.

Four large red ovate visor drones shot a barrage of continuous laser fire at her, she dodged and jumped and somersaulted around them without losing speed—never once getting hit. She jumped and held onto one of the drones.

With its ovalshape secured she used it to shoot three mini gel-discs that stuck on to each of the scattered, hovering machines. She leveraged herself with the drone and flipped over it landing with one leg raised behind her. She imagined it looked a lot like a stork stance. She landed a disc and leapt off the drone. The explosion behind her signaled the other three which exploded one after the other.

She landed on the Surface Road. She knew she couldn't stop there. She focused through the chaos and noticed snipers perched in the jungle trees with blasters. Senora dug underneath her shoulder guard and gripped a small metallic orb in her right hand. She ran faster this time and threw the pebble sized object. The red armored snipers of the Fifth Army, shot at her, but they weren't fast enough to keep up with a Kaiji Shinora. They missed. She passed the point where the small orb landed. Long cutting lasers shot from the orb into each of the sniper's helmets and eyecomm units. Whether human or reptilian *Algo Armossans,* didn't matter—both species, dead by lobotomy.

***

The massive Fortress door slid open allowing squadrons of troops armed with neon-lighted tremor swords and axes to rush through. They wore red and white metaplas: full torso, light armor with impact absorption panels.

Manalex's face appeared in the right upper corner of her contact lens.

"Senora, status."

"Thank you for chiming in." She dodged the incoming laser blasts. "I'm almost at the gate. Where are you?"

"I've killed over five thousand men in the north and west fortifications. The red brick walls of this fortress housed barracks all along the inside of it, you would think this place ancient."

"His technology, Brother. He's armed with some of the most modern weapons in the galaxy, some not even available in this system. And have you noticed? He's working with Reptilians now!"

"Yeah I noticed. Also, I'm impressed with how you reached the gate doing a mile and a half in under four minutes. I'm proud of you."

"Whatever—concentrate on your part of the mission Aly. I got the head man in charge."

"Senora, I told you not to call me that anymore—"

"Bye, Aly!" She switched off visual communications neurologically.

There were at least fifteen hundred men or more in front of her, securing the large metallic gate with the fifth army monogram etched on it.

She knew her brother would come through, no doubt. The galaxy's greatest assassin. He was highly skilled, a prodigy of sorts and next in line to bear the title of Soveranus. He had killed so many and she knew there would be many more deaths to come at his hands. His special-ized Simbiokinetik suit provided to him by his robotic sidekick, Wartik, turned him into a herald of death—almost impossible to defeat. The suit also gave him access to the mighty *OHM Swords,* the blade formed by the winds. OHM swords were built by the tribes of the *Alfi* Dwarves, a fusion between magic and technology.

Senora wasn't helpless. She had gained a reputation for some of the most brutal kills in the Blue Ocean, and the owner of the dreaded magical *Falaka daggers.* The daggers were made with a large inwardly curving, single-edged blade, concave near the point, convex near the iron hilt engraved with PaWa characters. The more blood got on them, the sharper they became, also courtesy of the *Alfi.*

Her victims feared her symphony just as much as they did her mur-derous weapons.

Her kill system called the *Symphony* was based on the beautiful dances she learned as a child, and she excelled at them. The squadrons standing before her were ready to maul and rend her to pieces, but she had her Symphony.

***

The roar and sound of battle cry was almost deafening, and to a lesser fighter, overwhelming to the point of breaking. But to Senora, a child of violence since the day she turned four, it was a thrill, exhilarat-ing, and raised her blood lust.

"Long-lived is our death, as long-lived as war itself. Long-live the MINIAN."

In mere seconds she had hundreds of men upon her trying to cut into her. She rose with her feet together, knees straight, lifting her heels and on the balls of her feet, bringing her arms gracefully over her head slicing two then leaving the ground by jumping off of both feet and landing on them at the same time, killing another two as she crouched bringing her arms back like two pairs of wings. Her face now a bloody mess. All she knew was the dance, her mission, and the taste of blood on her lips.

She hated the taste of blood, she always had. The first time she ever drew blood was anything but glorious, but a necessary discomfort. She grew to like seeing the blood of her enemies stain the battlegrounds. She knew these were all responsible for the evil in their land.

She roared and shrieked into her aggressors gutting them. Her armor was hardly green at that point, just black and red like her victims.

She kicked her legs out, crushing heel and foot, bringing her arms together, slicing in straight lines or circles, dancing her way past her foes, cutting and slashing, stomps and arm swings, turns and then the *Muiso Bird dance* which consisted of a deadly spin of her body, going into fast cuts, she became a blur. Guards and soldiers died by the dozens. Their heads and limbs littered the battleground. In a *Fuer Hoomanu,* she continued until she was surrounded by only three, two humans and one Algo.

The Reptilian hissed at her. His long black hair covered his huge, triangular head. His throat was covered with spiny, dark grey scales which formed into beards. Several groups of even longer spiny scales were located at the corners of the mouth, and the external ear openings.

"You're dead woman." They formed a circle around her. Her daggers glowed a red hue from having made contact with blood.

"Kill her!" The Armossan charged her.

***

She quickly raised her closed fist at the two and shot a powerful wave of sound which she called *The Leopards Roar* toward them. The blast all but destroyed their ear drums sending them to their knees screaming in panic and agony.

The Armossan tried to cut her shoulder. He was fast, but she was bathed in the power of the Essence and had heightened reflexes. She grappled the Armossan's hand and twisted her torso downward sending him over her shoulder and slamming him to the ground.

Lightning cracked overhead and Senora focused through the rain to see her attacker.

He jumped to his feet and roared at her over the boom of thunder.

Another flash, the raindrops streamed down her beautiful face. Two more flashes revealed the red *M* tattoo on the right side of her face. The daggers in her hand collapsed into small hilts which disappeared inside the small cargo pocket.

The Almossan dove forward for another cut. Senora gripped his hand, twisting it firmly while stepping to the side. She pushed his arm up until the shoulder dislodged causing his weapon to crash on the ground. With his short tremor sword, she decapitated him.

She placed her right hand on the large metal gate and concentrated all her energy against the door. Unable to withstand the full pressure of the Essence, the Gate exploded and collapsed.

"I'm in." She marched across the debris.

"Good. Welcome to the party."

"You ever notice how creepy your voice sounds when you wear the Simbiokinetic suit?"

"The pot calling the kettle black, Senora. You creep me out all the time."

"Ha-ha, very funny, Bunhaw."

"You called me a bunhaw? I'm going to talk to father about your tongue when we get back to post."

"You're full of jokes today. What's the status, Aly?"

"I'm close to the training center of the Fortress. Lots of nasty stuff here. This guy was building a huge army, and I'm not talking just for aesthetics—he was planning something big."

"Let me know when you take down the artillery emplacements, that way we can call down the ME's to rain hell on this craziness."

"Sure, no problem. Senora...listen. As I was heading toward the prison area, I—"

"What is it? What's wrong?"

"Well—look, I'm not alone. There were some people I had to rescue. When you get to it, brace yourself."

"Understood. Senora out."

She had to admit the marble walls were beautiful. The place was of a gorgeous design. She wasn't running as fast anymore. She wanted to be careful, of course, but she also just wanted to observe the beauty within the fortress.

Art was stored as high as the ceiling, the libraries housed a large collection of rare books and historical documents, including government documents of the ancient Star empire, as well as the Manusa and Gried dynasties.

Two guards with tremor spears protected two giant red pillars at the end of the hall.

Senora aimed for their heads. Both dropped immediately. Steel darts were one of her favorite weapons.

The next hall was narrow, but still filled with pictures of ancient battles and leaders. One even had the battle between the Fifth army of the Red River Dragon and the Mighty Deborai Champions. The painter had done a very good job with their historic interpretation of the event. "Aly..."

"I told you to stop calling me that."

"Yeah, sorry. This hall—it's going to take me under the fortress."

"Follow it past the small doors and through the narrow gate. You'll know when you get there. Shit—"

"You okay?"

"Gotta go. They're coming from all sides."

Senora ended the link. I better get this done; sounds like he needs backup, she thought.

She focused her energy to increase her vision in the dim hall. She heard gasps and labored breathing but couldn't see the source until the final turn in the long passageway.

What a nightmare...

Prisoners filled the cells. Their cheeks were sunken and their bones looked as if they would come through their skin at any moment. They were dying from malnutrition, scarred from torture... Their eyes were dull and looked hollow. She spotted what used to look like a military tattoo on one of them. All the males seemed to have one. Some held each other tighter, with what little strength they had left.

"Don't fear me." She searched for clues in the room. There was a rebellion, she thought. "Are you prisoners of war?"

Silence.

"...after losing to the Fifth army?"   The console was at the end of the depressing and gloomy dungeon. Her heart broke with every step she took, their faces would stick in her mind forever. She pulled from her jacket a small black leather chip. She pointed the burgundy colored sensor at the console. It beeped three times then the bright red energy diminished into the ground. The prisoners left their cells slowly at first. Senora punched through the console bending the metal inwards with a few sparks and a small fire as evidence of her rage.

She turned and motioned for them to follow her up the stairs.

"Go back through this hall and wait for me outside. There will be people here to help you. Go in a straight line and don't look back!"

One of them, who appeared to be the eldest and weakened from the abuse, smiled with a gesture of appreciation with hands open wide and his arms at shoulder length. She held his weak wrists in her hands and. "Please go, you're free now."

The youngest girl took the elder by his hand. Senora watched until they disappeared through the fortress.

***

Senora sprinted past the lasers coming from the walls. She somersaulted past until giant square razors rose from the ground. They were coming out of the walls and ceiling too. She moved faster, maneuvering around and over each trap. She finally came to stop in an area where the walls had small dragon statues lined up against them on each side. The first row of tens spewed flames. The next ten spit hot melting Chemicals. I could shoot them with explosive gels, but could ignite something worse, she thought.

Senora focused her energy into what was known as the *Leopards High*. She put all her power into her legs and cardiovascular systems. As she neared the statues she leapt higher than anyone ever has in any galactic sport or game. She was sure it broke human records, but no one would ever see. Her leg extended and broke through the door and into the giant palace.

In the center, a large Grey River Dragon statue sat perfectly sculpted. It looked frighteningly real standing at one hundred feet and in the center of a very large pool of water. Goth Manusa knelt in front of the throne.. He wore red and white ceremonial robes.

Above the throne a great white sign rested. Etched in gold Pawa characters was the inscription: "The Throne of Love and Justice."

Symbolic red seals decorated the white walls along with dragons and what looked like Mount Killers Edge.

His hands hid in the full-length sleeves.

A scar ran down his right cheek. His prominent jaw and squared-off chin would've made him attractive if he wasn't such a monster.

"You came to kill the wrong man." His deep voice echoed throughout the palace.

"How so?"

"I haven't done anything wrong. I took what was rightfully mine. This fortress belonged to my ancestors first."

"My brother has all but eliminated your soldiers, less pestilence to grieve the hearts of men."

"You killed my best, though. It was beautiful to see."

"There isn't a single console or monitor or holo in this room, how did you see?"

"It was a Symphony... a play. You fight with a wonderful rhythm. The tempo—it was a sight to see!"

Her hands glowed bright blue. "Are you ready to die?"

The palace chamber shook as a muffled explosion boomed in the distance.

"There goes artillery. There go your weapons. And with that—your life."

"You mean to kill an innocent man?"

Her laugh sounded hysterical as it echoed through the throne room. She was impressed and disgusted by this beast's delusion. "Innocent? Have you been to your Dungeons! Do you see what you have done to these people? Goth, you worm!"

"Their ancestors killed mine long before we did theirs Shinora, my ancestors!" He bared his teeth. "They raped our mothers in wars and killed my father's, this was coming to them. This—this land is mine!"

"One evil act does not justify another, these people are different we are living in peace time!"

"No!"

"Yes, Goth, you are guilty of crimes against humanity- "

"No!"

"And, with the power vested in me, by the government of Tiehrra and the creed of the Minian Shinora clan that derives from the ancient book of blades-"

"Noooo...!."

"I, Kaiji Senora Hunt of the MINIAN now sentence you to Death."

He pulled out a blaster from his robe just as Manalex burst through the side door of the throne room.

A dark plume of Smoke trailed behind the Minian warrior and filled the room. Two men hung on, but their hits bounced off his suit. He gripped their throats. With one in each hand, lifting them into the air he broke their necks.

"Senora! Let's go!"

She leapt toward Goth causing his blaster fire to miss. She punched a glowing fist through his heart.

His blood and organs exploded forth from the impact. Goth's eyes were wide in shock and surprise.

She pulled her arm back, blood and fragment on her hands.

As he collapsed to the ground a pool of blood leaked from the hole in his chest onto the throne room floor.

Manalex's hand pulled her. "Come on, Senora. Let's go."

He was longer wearing the Simbiokinetik suit, but in his regular uniform. His robot sidekick Wartik stood beside him.

"I do hate to be the bearer of bad news, but if we don't leave now—"

"I know, Wartik." Senora snorted. "The Tiehrrans security force will level the whole place with us inside."

"Let's go." Manalex pulled Senora through the hole he had made in the side of the Throne Room.

The walls of the castle flashed past them as they ran at full speed through the maze of hallways until they reached the slaves and prisoners outside. The Tiehrran Air Force screamed overhead as bombs deployed over the Fortress. A satellite Kion blast was sent hurling into it. Their secret warehouses underground completely destroyed. The site lay a complete and total ruin.

The Tiehrran rescue ships landed with food and medical supplies.

The slaves cheered and clapped with whatever strength they had left.

The elder joined the side of the warriors and their robot companion. Together, they watched the fireworks and allowed themselves some level of pleasure at the sight.

They destroyed the enemy as they had done many times before, and they felt good for the moment, but in the end as she watched the conflagration unfold, she couldn't help but think about what Goth had said to her.

It made her think about good and evil, right and wrong, and she could not help but wonder, if maybe, just maybe, there was some level of—innocence, some justification to Goth's actions. Maybe our actions as individuals, no matter how evil they might be, are unavoidably triggered by the actions of others. Who is, by claim or intention, ultimately good, and who in this endless universe is ultimately and irredeemably evil?

A Subtle Change
Christopher Buckley

All full and well aware were we
of how to travel time —
to look; not touch, the things we'd see,
to not commit such crime.

Well-schooled regarding butterflies
and risks of changing lines;
how one small death could magnify,
and woven threads untwine.

A simple misstep, off the path,
could alter what we've known:
disturb, temporal, all the math,
the way the years have flown.

We'd never know the gravity
of one worm under foot.
How it could turn, and the degree;
how the new world would look.

So extra care we always gave
to tip not there the scales...
to never traffic there engrave,
to always mark the trail.

Still yet, at times, it crossed my mind:
the wonders of "What if?"
Perhaps that one moth I could find,
to change things but a whiff...

A thing I swore I'd never do:
set dominoes to fall.
But if, by chance, they'd bring me you...
for that I'd risk it all.

Dopamine Precursors

Carl Fuerst

Lux Timer stepped off the bus, losing his balance and bouncing off fifth-shifters as they stumbled to their assigned work-skill improvement opportunities. He landed against the neon guard rail, where he paused and pretended to swat a mosquito on the back of his neck, in an attempt to hide the adjustments he made to his stim-drip. Even though drips weren't illegal anymore, it was still considered crude to fondle them in public.

He watched the bus pull away, its engine huffing acidic air through ientry valves, converting nitrogen into fuel, and expelling the leftovers out gutter-pipes in its back end. It lurched forward, taking almost half a block to gain enough speed to become airborne again.

The influx of phenylpropanolamine, MDPV, and mephedrone-- among other things--into Lux's bloodstream cooled the red-hot ball of rage that had been burning a hole in his chest all afternoon.

He joined the river of bodies; he felt good, like a single strand in the braided length of rope that tied the world to the universe. About ten minutes later he felt bad again and decided to take a break.

***

People outside the bar watched--or pretended to watch--the vid-papers that covered the outside walls of the place; frantic, looping clips, announcing gladiator matches, dog-fights, or offering to purchase the rights to residential assignments, no matter how rusted or lice-ridden they might be.

Lux pushed his way inside, where he picked out one of the many empty booths. A waiter made his way from table to table, refilling people's drinks with an automatic nozzle-gun attached to a tank strapped to his back. A bloody set of boot-prints ran from the sex-sim chamber towards an area somewhere in back.

Lux's ears hissed with the high-pitched interference of two-dozen stim-drips turned to their highest setting.

In places like this, people with empty reservoir glands cranked their drips all the way up, hoping to suck enough vapors to stay awake. For some, this practice provided an extra few hours before they had to buy an expensive refill injection. Others, less successful, slumped over their tables, drool-streams trickling from the corners of their mouths.

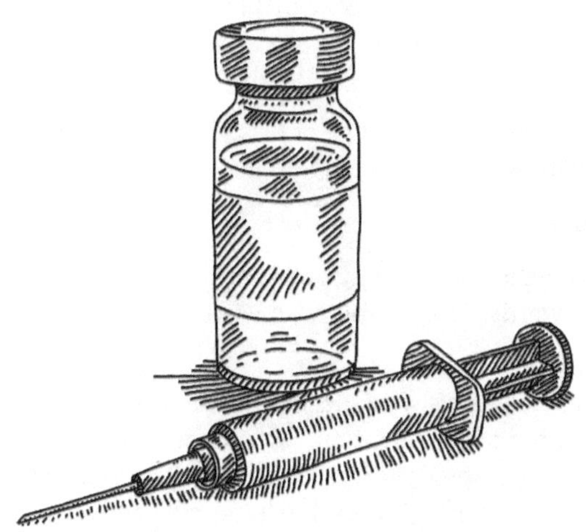

He saw Strong Coffee sitting at the long table that ran down the middle of the room. The skin under his eyes looked like wrinkled Bible-paper. His elongated body had a sick, fish-belly sheen, and he wore heavy rings with synthetic gems on all of his remaining fingers--two on one hand and three on the other. Since the Amputation-Code had passed, missing digits and limbs had become a symbol of authentic criminality. There were even places where you could have the wounds forged, for a fee.

Lux knew that Strong Coffee's wounds weren't forged.

He and Coffee had grown up together; they had traded parts for their first gliders, and roamed the alleys of their neighborhood after curfew. Then, Coffee's mom had gotten a life-sentence for chronic job-delinquency, back when that was still a crime, and things hadn't gone very well for Coffee since.

Lux had personally attended Coffee's first public amputation, which he'd earned for corporate slander and the willful tampering of his consumer freedom ID chip. He'd pleaded, "I'm sorry! I'm sorry!" the entire time.

Lux hadn't heard him say the words since.

Coffee had two drinks in front of him, and it looked like he was thinking hard about which one to take a sip of next. He grinned as Lux walked up to his table.

"What's cooking?" He slid one of his cups towards Lux. It was empty. Lux flagged down the waiter for a refill.

"Got fired today."

"*You*?" Coffee let out a long, wheezing laugh that seemed to make him tired afterwards. "That's *great*. Now you can finally start your adult life."

Coffee had traded his work-permit for three tabs of coitizone, two days after eighth-grade graduation. Lux had held on to his though, and it had paid off when they offered him two shifts a week at a plant that made safety-gauges for high-pressure lithium dispensers.

For over a decade, Lux hunched over a tiny desk with a pair of tweezers in each hand, twisting two small wires together on gauges and then dropping them down a chute for further processing. While he never quite figured out what those wires did, he did find great comfort in an income that kept him in dry sleeping quarters and a reliable supply of stim.

"What'd you do? Connect the wrong wires?"

"They sprung two extra shifts on me for no reason. I guess half the sixth-shift crews got arrested last night, and they wanted to make a big show about how we didn't need them around anymore."

"That's why I've avoided those situations my whole life. You're just not in control! They find a guy stealing Funemas from a pharmacy half way across the world and you're stuck feeling the effects."

Lux tapped his fingers on the table. "I don't know what to do."

"So, two extra shifts."

"Yup."

"That's what? Three extra hours?"

"Near the end of it, I asked to go to the bathroom, and they said, 'Go ahead, and don't ever come back.' They confiscated my work permit, too."

"That's hard," said Coffee. He grinned and finished another drink.

Lux ordered some jellyfish, and the waiter brought it out almost immediately. While Lux ate his food, Coffee excused himself to flirt with the half-dozen prostitutes leaning against the bar. One of them had won the talent competition at their school when they were very young; Lux remembered that she had been very good at jumping rope.

Three men came in, looked around the place, and went directly to Lux's table. Like Coffee, their hands were low on fingers; two of them even had clipped ears. They wore the kind of suits you could only buy--at exorbitant prices--from the vending machines that lined the streets in the rich parts of the city.

You were supposed to wear those once and then throw them away.

These men had obviously been trying to extend the lifespan of their outfits; they were torn at the knees, and the colors had swirled into each other to form a queasy looking gray.

They sat down.

After the water brought a fresh round of drinks, one man said: "Heard about your job, Lux. That's too bad."

"Yup," said Lux.

"Seen Trance?"

"Nope."

"We've got work for him. Nothing serious. He's just got to stand in a certain place, at a certain time, and get seen by certain people, while something else happens, somewhere else."

"Sounds about up to Trance's abilities," said Lux. "But I haven't seen him around."

"We like you, Lux. Even more than that, we *trust* you. Do you trust us?"

"I'm not Trance, man."

"What's that supposed to mean? I'm sitting here, looking at you. I'm, like, looking at you straight in the face. I'm talking to *you,* not Trance."

"I don't do that kind of work, is all I'm saying."

"I didn't offer you a job, Timer. Christ, I didn't even offer you an *interview* for the job. No, man, no, I'm looking for Trance. He's the man we need."

"If I see him, I'll tell him."

"I know."

Lux watched them leave.

He told himself to feel sorry for them. He'd grown up with those men, too. He'd grown up with everybody, and seen everybody's parents send them out to scrape up credits any way they could. He'd seen the scars everyone had received when they failed; in many ways, they were worse than the Amputation-Code could ever inflict. He'd seen the work dwindle and disappear, until it felt like the planet itself had slept in until one in the afternoon and was now stumbling around its apartment feeling guilty, because nobody had noticed, and because it had nothing to rush off to, nothing important to do.

Lux scanned his bill and transmitted the credits to the register. The meal and drinks just about cleaned him out.

He went outside where workers in mint-condition coveralls rushed to the depot, where the bigger companies sometimes rounded up volunteers. Lux pretended to swat another mosquito, but his stim reservoir was hopelessly dry. The three men in disposable clothes were across the street, chatting with a vendor as she ladled steaming bowls of caffeinated fish broth. He was already getting drowsy, and he didn't have enough for a refill.

Lux turned in their direction; he hardly had enough for a bowl of that filthy broth.

***

When Strong Coffee discovered that Lux had already left, his eyes darted nervously to the door. He let out a long, dry, humorless wheeze, started towards the exit, stopped, and sank down into his seat.

"It's about time something happened to somebody *else*," he said to the former jump-rope champion, who plopped down in his lap. He looked at his sawed-off knuckles, and she told him to buy her a drink. She pretended not to notice his dark mood, and Coffee pretended to forget what was making him so upset. It wasn't hard to do.

In fact, that was pretty much all everyone did, every long day of their lives.

Why I Like Boogler's Splendarium
Carl Nelson

First off, there's all sorts of neat stuff.
So it's not just the story that happens -
it all happens!
Force and energy shields, gravity wheels,`
are all mythopoesis in the hybrid structarium
of the multispec novel of interstellar disruption.

The milky fluids, snaking tubes,
metal cylinders and fusion pumps
perform feats of magic on the male brain
with conjuring words like
'ancient Archesonorum mind control',
and actual tools like the hyperspanner,
whose mental aptitude combined
with tri-dimensional portal adjusters
would make it a great side-kick
and the smartest wrench
you'd ever slip into your work belt.

Suns collapse, moons explode,
my lover goes from green to lavender
when she's been satisfied
and swims away,
vanishing into the plenthorum.
"So, we're good?"
I think we're good.

Further down the bookstore shelf,
are the spines of worlds yet undreamed of.
My eyesight is fast as the speed of light,
which is actually quite slow
compared with the speed of concept.

Light is so four-dimensional that
the fifth, sixth and seventh dimensions
can literally bore holes in it!

What we so readily perceive as reality
is really so much Swiss cheese!

There are so many dimensions,
parallel universes and such,
that holding down our own
is usually presented
as the major fictional difficulty...
as first described in
Boogler's Second Brackett Equation.

$$\Sigma F = \rho Q\left(V_{out} - V_{in}\right)$$

His First Equation established
the Boogler Splendarium.
The Second specified the forces
which anchor our place in it.
Fairies and unicorns are Fantasy--not allowed
due to strict limitations,
derived from the Bracket Equation.

The Android Commentaries are an effort
to bridge this gulf,
but I don't see it happening...
not in this year 1230 of the Post Illumination.

Mulded

Paul Stansbury

Hack leaned on the counter, watching the late afternoon heat shimmer off the flat, parched ground. The motor of the refrigerator chest hummed, laboring to keep the beer cold in the searing Arizona summer heat. A rolling ball of dust moved swiftly up the road. When it got close enough, Hack could see it was one of the fancy Wrangler JK's they rented back in Dooley to adventurers from the city who wanted to rough it in comfort. It slowed, pulling off the road into the gravel parking lot, tires scrunching as it came to a stop. Some dust, not willing to give up the chase, wafted past the Wrangler toward the screen door and front windows of the weather-beaten building.

A young man hopped out of the Jeep, pulled out his cell phone and took a selfie before following the dust through the door. He squinted as he looked around the interior of the store. There were a few old tables in the center, banked on either side by glass display cases, and an old time saloon bar ran across the back of the store.

"Is this Mulded, mister?" the young man asked.

"It's pronounced Mule Dead," answered Hack. "Story is that Elmore Shouse came here in 1880 lookin' for gold. He had jus' found some when his mule up and died. Thought that would be a good name for the place. Apparently, he weren't much of a speller cause when he filed his claim, he wrote out Mulded. The name stuck. Turns out his claim petered out right fast, so he decided there was more money to be made in selling whisky, beans and shovels to the would-be miners. Anyways, that's how the story goes. I'm Hack, young feller. What they call you?"

"My name's Leland Lowe; I'm an amateur ufologist. I've been over to Roswell, Alamogordo, White Sands and Spaceport America. Before I leave for Area 51, thought I'd check out the place where the Mulded Maiden incident took place. Is this it?"

"Sure is. Back in 1955; I was here."

"You're telling me you were there when she landed? How do I know this isn't just some yarn you tell tourists to sell a few trinkets?"

"See for your own self." Hack turned and grabbed a large picture frame from amid the bottles on the shelf. He took a towel and gently wiped the dust from the glass, then studied it a moment before laying it on the counter.

Leland walked up to the bar. The picture frame contained a yellowed newspaper clipping. The heading read: **Local Men Claim Female Alien Visits Local Grocery!** Beneath it was a grainy photograph of several men in front of the very bar where he was now standing.

"Don't hardly seem like it was sixty three years ago," said Hack. "I was sixteen. Ed Spivey owned the store back then. He'd got it from Elmore Shouse himself, and when he died, he give the store to me." Hack tapped a gnarled finger on a boyish face in the photo. "That's me right there. We posed for the reporter from the Dooley Sentinel who come down to get our story. I'm the only one left. All the others have passed on." He wiped at his eyes with a bar towel. "Do you see the name 'Hack Boyd' underneath the photo? That's me. How 'bout somethin' to drink while you read the article?"

"Sure," said Leland. "What do you have on tap?"

"Nada. All I got is Miller or Bud - in longnecks."

"Let me have a Bud."

"How about a burger to go with that?" asked Hack.

"Do you have a menu?"

"Nope. Jus' with or without."

"With or without what?" asked Leland.

"Cheese."

"With."

"You get chips with that. Pick a bag from the rack," Hack said.

He pulled a longneck from the cooler and laid it on its side, rolling it across a stack of napkin-like papers, neatly covering the slippery sides.

He inserted the bottle in an opener mounted on the end of the counter and popped off its cap, which fell with a soft clinking noise into a can below. He placed the beer on the bar in front of Leland, then walked over to a dingy refrigerator and retrieved a stack of hamburger patties from the freezer and a pack of sliced cheese.

He turned on the gas to the flattop and tossed on a patty.

"It'll take a bit for the flattop to warm up." Hack said.

"Not much left around here but the store, I see," said Leland.

"Yeah, the rest moved out years ago."

Leland took a draw on his longneck. "I take it they thought you all were pulling a hoax. So, tell me what really happened."

"Well, let me start out by saying all that Mulded Maiden stuff is a bunch of hooey, made up by some shady businessmen up in Dooley. Thought they could make this thing into a big money makin' tourist attraction. After a while, the story got so outlandish, no one believed it and it all blew up in their faces. Only, we were the ones forever branded as hoaxers."

"Got to expect stuff like that if you're going to go around claiming female aliens stopped by."

"It ain't a claim. It happened, and it was only the one."

 Leland took another draw on his longneck. "Well, I'm listenin', at least until my burger's done."

Hack studied the young man for a moment before starting. "Well, it was late in the afternoon on a Saturday jus' about this time of year. The Morgan twins, Bob Wiley and big Frank Peavey, were already here when I arrived. Ed was frying up burgers. I ordered one and got a cream soda out of the cooler. 'Ida Red Likes The Boogie' by Bob Wills was playing on the jukebox. I had no sooner sat down when this loud rumbling noise commenced and the whole place started to shake. Bob shouted, 'Earthquake!', and we all headed for the door, stumblin' out into the parking lot."

"That's when the mothership landed?" asked Leland.

"Weren't no mothership," growled Hack. "That's one of them lies those boys in Dooley made up; it's stuff like that, made us a laughin' stock. Anyhoo, we got out to the parkin' lot jus' in time to see the strangest thing. It looked like one of them fancy hydroplane racing boats, but it wasn't in no water. It was floatin' down out of the sky, all smooth and shiny silver colored. Then it jus' hovered about a foot above the ground. By then, all the rumblin' and shakin' had stopped. It had a canopy of sorts on top which slid open and the most beautiful gal you ever saw got out."

"So let me get this straight," asked Leland, "a galactic race boat flew down from the sky and the most beautiful woman you ever saw got out?"

"Does a coyote crap in the cottonwoods? You bet your life, that's jus' what happened . . ."

***

Hack stood alongside the others in the dusty parking lot, staring at the woman who had just emerged from the sleek silver machine. She was tall, with curly chestnut hair, lavender eyes, and a nice figure. Despite the fact that she had just dropped out of the sky, her friendly smile immediately put Hack at ease.

"My name is Aubrina," she said. "You boys got anything cold to drink? Flying across the galaxy sure makes a girl thirsty. I could do with something to eat, too."

Ed led her into the store. "How about a Miller," he said, searching under the bar for a glass. "Ain't fancy, but they do call it the champagne of bottled beer."

"What more could a girl ask for?" laughed Aubrina.

Ed looked in the refrigerator. "Humph. . . as for somethin' to eat, I can cook you up a cheeseburger or I got some chicken salad if it ain't gone bad."

"Cheeseburger. You got a music maker in this place?"

Ed pointed to the jukebox. "I'll get some quarters from the register," he said.

"Don't worry, I got it," she said, waving her hand. The jukebox started right up.

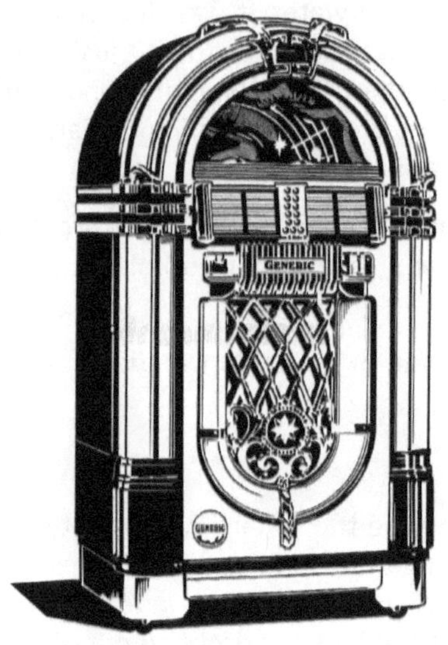

". . . Hell," Hack said, shaking his head, "we pushed back the tables and took turns doing the two-step with her. When she wasn't dancin' or singin', she was eatin' cheeseburgers. Must'a ate half a dozen. She would sing softly in your ear when you held her close. She smelled like the white desert wildflowers that pop up in the spring. An' she was light as a ball of cotton and just as soft. She kept that old jukebox playin' most of the night while we all took turns dancin' with her. The thing was, it seemed like it didn't make no difference to her that we was jus' ordinary fellers. She jus' made you feel good. I fell in love with her that night. We all did . . ."

***

Hack held Aubrina closely as she sang the last refrain of 'The Tennessee Waltz' in his ear. It was 3 am. "Boys, I hate to say it, but it's time for me to go," she said. "I've had a wonderful time."

***

". . . with that, she waved her hand," said Hack, "and the jukebox fell silent. She asked Ed to fix her a cheeseburger to go, and the rest of us walked out into the parking lot with her. She motioned toward her ship and the canopy slid back. Along about then, Ed came rushing up and handed her a sack with her cheeseburger in it. She gave us all a hug and a kiss on the cheek, then she hopped back in her machine. Everything rumbled and shook again before it shot straight up, disappearing into the starry night sky."

Hack checked the burger which had begun to sizzle. He smashed it down with his spatula, then flipped it over. He retrieved a sack of buns from atop the refrigerator, before unwrapping a slice of American and depositing it on the burger.

Leland waited until Hack was finished.

"So that's the story? A beautiful woman flies down to Earth and you guys spend the night drinking beers and dancing to the jukebox. You fall in love with her, then you send her off into the night sky with a cheeseburger! I've got to say that's a hard sell, even for the 50's."

"Can't change what happened cause folks is expectin' to hear something different," said Hack. "You want any mustard or catsup on your burger? Got some dill pickles, too."

"Just some mustard."

Hack grabbed the cheeseburger and a squeeze bottle of mustard, and set them on the bar in front of Leland. He paused for a moment, then tossed two more patties on the flattop.

"Maybe I should get this to go," said Leland.

"Stay where you are kid," said Hack. "Enjoy your cheeseburger. You ain't hurt nobody's feelings."

"Does the jukebox work?" asked Leland.

"It's temperamental," said Hack. He fished a quarter out of the register and tossed it on the bar.

Leland walked over to the jukebox. "This is an antique," he said.

"Same one that was here in '55."

Leland wiped the dust from the glass and peered at the song selections. "These songs are antiques too."

"Ed never wanted any others after that night; neither did I."

Leland put the quarter in the slot. It clinked through the chutes and dropped into the coin box with a muffled clink. "What's a good one?"

"I like 'em all, but I'm partial to 'The Tennessee Waltz'."

Leland searched the playlist until he found it, and pushed the button. No response. He tried it again. Same result. He tried a different song, then another. The jukebox remained silent. Instead, he heard a soft rumbling in the distance. It was growing louder, and as it grew, the windows began to rattle.

Hack stepped out from behind the bar and made a beeline for the door. "Better get a move on boy, or you'll miss out."

"Miss out on what?"

"Not what. Her, stupid! The female alien, The Mulded Maiden, Aubrina."

"No way I'm falling for that," Leland called out. The rumbling was increasing. "It's got to be a helicopter or something."

"Suit yourself," Hack yelled back through the screen door.

Leland could feel the rumble in his chest. "Wait for me!" He bolted for the door and found Hack standing in a whorl of dust, looking up and waving his hand. Leland joined him as a ruby red craft descended.

The rumbling and shaking faded away. As the dust was carried off by the early evening breeze, Leland could see the ship was floating motionless, about a foot above the gravel.

The canopy slid back and the most beautiful woman he had ever seen stepped out.

"That can't be her, can it?"

"Sure is," said Hack. "She ain't changed a bit since I first saw her."

"I thought you said her ship was silver."

"Oh, she changes the color of that thing like she changes her nail polish," laughed Hack.

***

Aubrina, Hack, and Leland ate cheeseburgers, drank beer and danced until the wee hours of the morning. Patti Page was singing the last refrain of 'The Tennessee Waltz' when Aubrina said, "I hate to say it boys, but it's time for me to go. I had a swell time."

Hack and Leland walked her to the spaceship. She gave Leland a kiss on the cheek. "It was my pleasure to meet you."

"The pleasure was all mine," he said.

Aubrina motioned to her ship, and the canopy slid back.

She took Hack's face in her hands, kissed him on the forehead, hugged him, then stepped back and looked into his eyes. A tear rolled down her cheek.

"Hack, you're dying," she whispered.

"Yeah, the docs say it won't be long," he said.

"Such fragile creatures your kind are. You bloom like spring flowers, then you are gone."

"Oh, I've had a good run. I danced with the Mulded Maiden, you know." Hack fell silent for a moment. "You got room in that thing for two?" he asked.

"Yes."

He held up a sack. "Got a couple of cheeseburgers to go. I was wonderin' if you would take me up there with you for a spell, like you done with the others." He looked up at the sky.

"I've always wanted to see what it's like and this is likely my last chance. As you know, it probably won't turn out to be a very long ride."

"I know," said Aubrina. She took his hand and led him up to the canopy. When they reached the opening, Hack turned, fished a ring of keys from his pocket, and tossed them to Leland.

"What's this for?" the younger man asked.

"The store is yours, kid, if you want it; I got no use for it now. Everything you need to know is written on the side of the refrigerator. If you're smart, you won't say anything about tonight . . . and don't fret, she'll stop by and see you again one day."

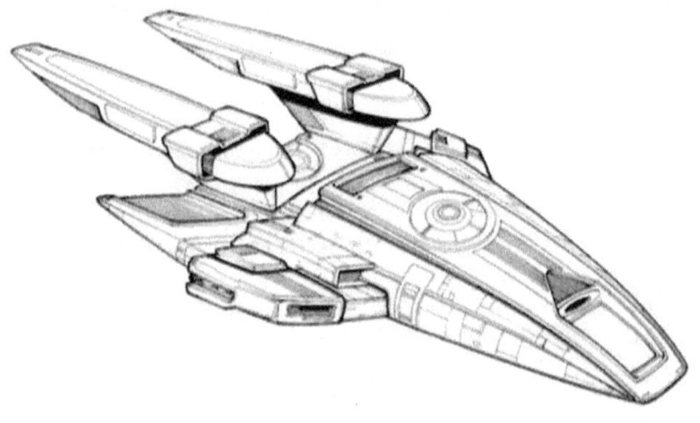

Adrift

Christopher Buckley

It's cold and lonely here in space;
the icy tendrils on my face.
That grow and reach to scratch and claw,
to tatter heart's flesh; rent and raw,
and freeze the tears this pain's unlaced.

Though left, I did: trained, steeled and braced,
'twas unprepared for hunt and chase
of ghosts of you — their pitch and yaw,
in this cold and lonely...

Here lost and stranded with no trace,
with little hope of reaching base...
Yet's not the last of breath I'll draw,
not eclipsed sun, nor shadow's maw,
that grip and stifle screams encased...
in this cold and lonely.

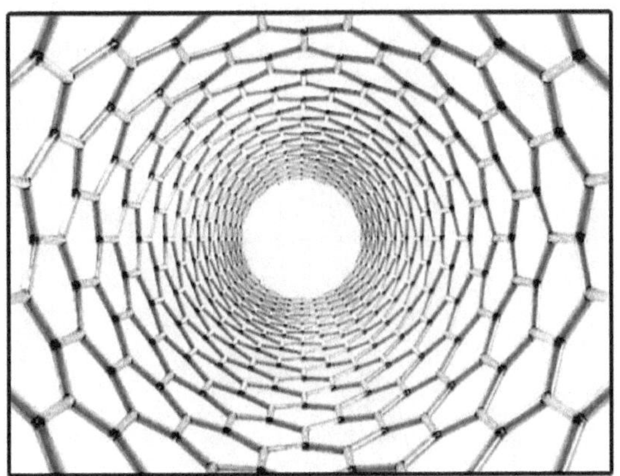

The Old Man's Song

Isabella Ann Gaines

Every year when the carnival comes to town, Clef's Piano Bar gets a lot of interesting customers. Clowns, bearded ladies, kids with masks of face paint, ringmasters--you name it, we see it. However, despite all of the eccentricities that walk through the door, there's one strange encounter that will always stick out in my mind.

It was a normal Tuesday night at the bar, and I was warming up on the piano with some simple scales and arpeggios before the dinner rush came in. I was eager to try out a new piece I had been working on to entertain our guests; I always liked to impress creative people, such as the carnies.

I'd had a bit of a controversy with my manager earlier that evening, but he had eventually allowed me to perform the new piece, even though he usually made me stick to the predetermined score.

The metronome clicked on as my fingers twirled up and down the keys as if in an elegant ballroom dance. I hated that darned metronome, with its old, slow gears caused by years of oxidation. It constantly caused me to delay my performances, in order to fiddle with it. I always had to set it way above tempo, just so the elderly needle would get to the next click on time.

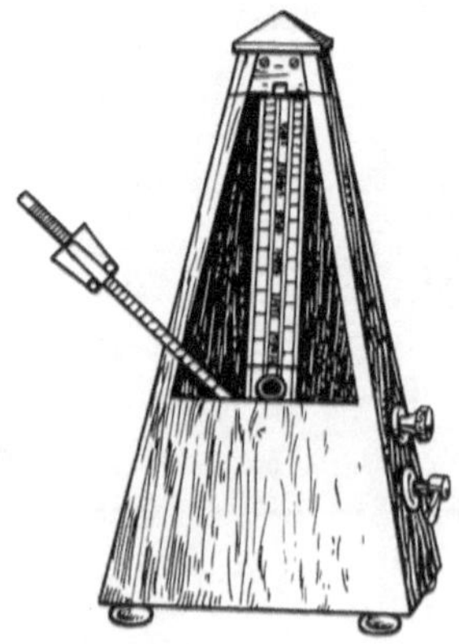

I'd considered buying a new one, but the boss seemed to have an attachment to the thing, and I knew better than to get into another juvenile row with him.

Just as I was setting up to play the first song--a lively tune I knew by heart--an old, familiar looking gentleman with a sprained ankle came walking up to me. I smiled at him, and pointed to the donation box on top of the piano.

"If you would like to make a song request, the fee is $5. All of the proceeds go to local charities."

"I would pay you if I could, but I only have this," he said somber-ly, pulling an apple out of his coat pocket and setting it in the basket. "Please, sir, you must play me this song; it means the world to me."

The man handed me a sheet of music titled *Sassafras Waltz*. It was an awkward tune, marked in 6/8 time, and I had never heard of it be-fore, despite my vast knowledge of suites. I opened my mouth to po-litely decline, but something in his face made me feel for him. His eyes sparkled with longing, like those of someone who had just lost their spouse, and only wanted to hear their voice again. Perhaps this song was of the same significance to him, and hearing it would ease whatev-er kind of grief he was feeling.

I looked over the piece before slowly starting off. I stumbled quite a bit, apologizing every time. I did such a poor job that some people be-gan getting up and leaving. My manager was certainly not happy with my performance. The old man, however, looked very happy; I couldn't help but feel he had been in my shoes before and was proud of me for trying.

Once I finished the song, he thanked me with a shaky handshake and a kiss to the cheek, and left.

I never saw the man again, but he left behind the sheet music; today it is my favorite piece of music I have ever played. I only wish that my old, arthritic hands were nimble enough to dance on the keys, and my poor, aching ankle was strong enough to hold the pedals; I would dearly love to hear it played one last time.

Finding Megalodon
Richard King Perkins II

One never knows
when a giant tentacle will reach up
from out of the sea—
like that object that crept up from water
which might be bleak discovery;
quite out of place in the arid world,
so that if we didn't know better,
we might call it archaic hammerhead,
or plesiosaur or even megalodon—
but we know it cannot be these things,
so we rename our find, calling it cryptozoic.

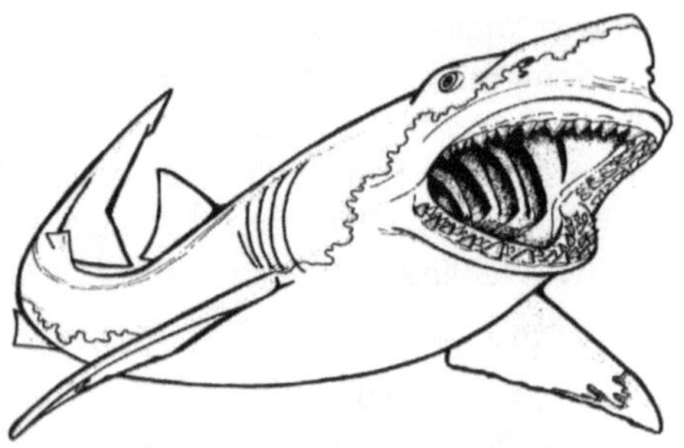

Seen against the illicit horizon,
its appearance changes with each
slashing grasp of water—
and our conviction wavers as well,
so we rename our passenger,
calling it hateful and vile.

Looking for another existence
and the remainder of the world,
we found something flourishing
at the bottom of a decayed, thieving ocean—
the fossil-lives of recognizable creatures
kept in the immutable state
which we would likely call horrific.

Slim Slow Slider

David Perlmutter

I.

I was a bit of a late adapter when it came to the newfangled technologies the humans brought into our universe. I was, after all, born and bred in the *twentieth* century, when you couldn't possibly carry a phone in your pants pocket, 'cause it was too heavy. But then it got to the point that conducting my one-person medical practice meant I couldn't duck-and-cover anymore.

It wasn't all that long ago the idea of a female doctor would have caused suspicion, but times have changed. I have a website and a blog now, but I'll be damned if I'll have one of those stupid "smartphones" on me. I'm not *that* kind of doctor. You can call me at the office, or at home, but nowhere in between--at least as long as they let me keep my landlines.

It wasn't much of a surprise, or an inconvenience, when I got that phone call; it was just a bit of a shock to hear what I was addressed as.

"You out there, Slim Slow Slider?" said a familiar voice, calling me to a duty I hadn't expected to be called to. Not for a while, anyway.

Members of the Cartoon Republican Army--in which I hold the rank of Major--have to resort to addressing themselves in phone conversations by code names, since the American government is notoriously over-observant when it comes to suspected "bad guys" like us. So when I had to come up with a code name; it ended up being a name I was tagged with as a young scrub, owing to my affection for that mysterious and spiritually aware Irishman, Van Morrison, and his album *Astral Weeks,* of which "Slim Slow Slider" is the last, shortest and arguably most intimate track. It seemed like that's what people should call me if I couldn't be addressed by my right name.

I was at the office when I got the call, so I knew it was business. The calls I get there are that kind, unlike at home.

"You got her," I said.

"Good. This is Big F."

A.k.a. Field Commander, the number two person in the whole CRA, and the one who directly runs most of our operations. I knew this wasn't a social call, so I responded accordingly.

"What's the score, F?" I asked. "Why call this humble little physician, and not one of your bigger guns?"

"Because this problem is in your territory. And I can't get in touch with anyone else in town."

"Blame the humans. Nobody can get a cell signal outside the city anymore."

"Then how come I'm talking to you?"

"I don't have a cell--just landlines. There's still the potential they'll tap the lines, but they do that a lot less often than they used to."

"Well, you better get prepared to make a house call, Doctor. The humans are planning to go on the warpath again."

"When are they *not* doing that?"

"I'm serious. When the deal goes down, there will assuredly be casualties. Colonel Doe is doing an indoctrination session for some new recruits at the O-Town Hilton, and the humans are going to try to snuff them out with some sort of incendiary or explosive device."

"What?"

Fire is the one true weakness that we animated cartoon characters all have. Get any flame near our bodies and they burn up quick, like meat on a spit. We've taken to wearing flame retardant clothes on duty as a precaution, but not all of us can afford that stuff, and those who can't are the ones who usually bite it when trouble happens.

"How much time have I got?" I said. "I'm at the office right now, and the Hilton's on the other side of town."

"You should make it in time, if you get going," she said.

"That I will," I responded, narrowing my eyes as I spoke.

Hanging up, I retrieved my old reliable Gladstone bag and prepared for battle, by loading it with the tools and supplies I might possibly need.

II.

It had been a long journey to that point in my life, and I'd had to deal with some rough stuff--things which had tested me more than anything that might happen at the hotel.

My mother, for one thing. She hadn't wanted me to take the Hippocratic Oath to start with. She would've preferred that her Paula be like all the rest of the compliant, submissive lady cats the Hutchinson clan had produced before I came along--but I inherited my dad's stubbornness and will power, and fought back. I made it through medical school with flying colors, and then was able to set myself up in private practice as a GP, right after I finished training as an intern. I knew I didn't have any place in our city's one badly run hospital; I had my ethics to consider.

Then there's the hook. Everyone wants to know about it when they meet me for the first time; there aren't many MDs with an artificial limb, even among us 'toons. Since I'm right-handed, the hook on my left isn't much of an impediment to doing my job.

I didn't lose it intentionally, of course; when I was still just a scrub, I was working with a lady crocodile who didn't like the natural perkiness I tend to exude--even when I don't mean to--and bit it clean off. The blood loss made me pass out immediately, so it wasn't until I woke up that I found I had a hook for a left hand. Apparently, they had no actual artificial hands in storage in the supply room--or so they *said*.

Not that it stopped me, of course.

All it meant was that particular hospital would have one less doctor; I was sure about that particular fact.

Well, it also meant that I ended up being called "Captain Hook" or "Dr. Hook" a lot, which naturally increased when I joined the CRA. Usually among the members who are my age or older.

The younger ones are a bit more deferential, now that I've come into the more matronly phase of my life. They typically just call me "Dr. Hutchinson", or just plain "Doc". Only my good friends, contemporaries and patients of long standing address me as "Paula", and there aren't as many of those as there used to be, since things got weird.

By that, of course, I mean what's happened between us so-called "cartoon characters" and the humans in America.

It started when they figured out we weren't just figures they had "created" for "television programs", and actually posed a security threat. They decided to relocate us all in a ridiculous mass abduction, to a small, sub-orbital rock in space known as Orthicon. We might have gone by our own free will, at least some of us, if they'd *asked* us, but we all know the humans--or their military, anyhow--have no manners; they just shipped us there at gunpoint.

You don't forget being intimidated like that--even if it turns out their weapons can't actually kill you.

That's how the CRA started--a desire for revenge, and for some it was a chance to do illegal and sadistic things, without fear of injury, death or persecution. The humans found out what we could do when we got pushed too far. California is going to take a long time to recover.

They have the nerve to call *us* monsters 'cause of what we did to them, or what they *thought* we had been doing to their kids in the old days on the TV. That's all we are to them; they refuse to acknowledge that we have the same minds and personalities they do.

They're the *real* monsters here.

On Orthicon, I was one of the few 'toon doctors, and certainly the only GP, so I was able to get a lot of work--and a lot of money. Even when I insisted I didn't want to be paid, they shoved dollars and scrip and IOUs in my face like crazy. When it was all over--after we rebelled and demanded to go back to our old homes, and they finally obliged--I was better off financially than some of the other folks who had gone from living protected Hollywood lives, to searing desperation over-night. There'd been cases like that before Orthicon and the CRA, sure, but back then we had to grin and bear it. Not like now.

The trouble was, Americans didn't trust us to run our own affairs anymore--as if they *ever* had. Those cities of ours that hadn't been snuffed out of existence in the aftermath of Orthicon--thankfully, O-Town was one of these--still have American soldiers up their rear ends, "running" things "for" us.

Imagine being on the losing end of a fight, and having the victors rub it in your face by occupying your territory. That's how it is for us now. We can live and work as we please, provided we don't do or say anything the Americans don't like. Which is to say, *everything*.

A lot of my acquaintances who resettled on Earth after they lost their homes, want me to come to Earth and be involved in the CRA full-time, but I keep refusing them. I have my practice to maintain, and I still believe in the old place, even though it's as much of an urban death trap as any American city when the sun goes down.

Besides, *somebody* has to provide affordable health care in this city, and I do the best I can to do just that.

III.

When I finished loading the Gladstone, I dropped it on the seat next to me, and drove downtown towards the hotel. I heard the sound of the explosion the same as everyone else did, even with the windows rolled up. Most of the crowd around me on the parkway stopped dead in their tracks. Given how much weird crap happens around here, you'd think they'd be used to it, but they still behave like anyone whose normal routine was disrupted. All it meant for me, though, was that the need for my services had probably arisen, as the Field Commander had warned. I found a free lane, shifted to first gear, and motored my way to the Hilton.

The humans arrived before I did, and cordoned off the area. From what I could see from my car, the explosion hadn't occurred on one of the numerous upper floors, but on the main floor where, among other things, the conference center and ballrooms were.

I'd been here plenty of times on business, so I knew it would have been in one of those rooms where it happened; it was there I would have to go.

I parked, got out of the car, and walked towards the hotel. A soldier, dressed in one of those metal suits they wear for "protection" from us-- although it's never done them any good--got in my path and demanded I state my business.

"I should think that *that* would be obvious," I said, gesturing to the Gladstone with my good hand. It became just as obvious, he wasn't familiar with medicine practiced on a freelance basis, when he asked me to explain further.

"I'm a *doctor*," I said. "I came here to do my *job*. 'K? This city's not as big as you might think, and I easily could have some of my regular patients in there. So, if you don't mind. . ."

"I don't believe you," he answered.

"*What?*"

"You could easily be one of those animated *quacks*."

I bristled at his umbrage. No legitimate doctor wants to be called the "q" word. Especially not one who was legitimately trained and licensed to practice, and had fought a tooth-and-nail battle to be respected as a professional female healer. The fact that the vast majority of animated physicians aren't exactly . . . competent . . . had probably colored his thinking. He had the nerve to consider me one of *them*.

I could have gotten mad and started yelling at him, but I knew the humans thought all of us 'toon girls were loudmouthed harridans, even if it we really weren't, and I'd just be confirming a particularly odious stereotype if I acted that way.

I whipped off the glove from my hook. The soldier was shocked, like he'd never seen one before.

"Here's how it'll be," I said, gritting my teeth. "You are going to let me inside to practice my profession on the fellow members of my race who need my help, and I *won't* have to use this thing to cut you open like a *can!* Trust me. I've done it to bigger fellows than you, wearing that pathetic get-up. It would really be worth your while to *not* let me do the *opposite* of what I was trained to do, on you, *right now! Got it?!*"

He did, and he let me pass. I don't know what I would have done to him, or vice versa, if he hadn't, but he didn't force me to consider that option.

Fortunately, I had no more trouble. The other soldiers seemed to know a doctor when they saw one, and none tried to stop me. One even kindly let me know exactly where the incident had happened, so I wouldn't go to the wrong place by accident.

When I saw what had happened, I wished--though only for a second--that I had.

The room smelled positively acrid, with the odor of gunpowder lingering in the air. The back of the room--windows, wallpaper, walls, masonry and all--had been completely torn apart, but the damage seemed to have been limited to that area. Any fire that might have occurred had been prevented by the floors being lacquered and without carpeting, as they were in the whole place. That was likely how everybody got hurt, diving down abruptly on orders to "hit the deck" when the explosion happened. There were 'toons splayed out across the floor, nursing various kinds of wounds to their bodies.

There didn't seem to be a lot of people I knew. Since they all wore the red arm bands typically worn by CRA members on duty, they were likely new recruits to the cause.

Fortunately, there was one face I did recognize, for she was one of my regular, long-standing patients. I went to her immediately; that she seemed to be choking on something, hastened my pace.

I grabbed Jane Doe by her hair with my good hand and elbowed her sharply in the stomach with my hooked one. The offending item--a brick, probably loosened from the wall by the explosion's force--flew out, and plunked itself on the floor somewhere out of my sight, but not, judging by the shout coming from the corner afterwards, before it hit someone on the head.

Jane got up, picked up her blue beret, dusted it off on her matching blue coat, put it on her head, and stared at me.

"Thank you, Paula," she said. "I nearly bought it there, huh?"

"You're lucky you didn't get yourself burned, Colonel," I answered.

"It wasn't like that. It was a smoke bomb. It filled the whole room after it blew up. We upset the tables and chairs, and ended up flinging around in the darkness until we smacked into each other and fell down. I was over there at the podium, conducting the meeting, when it hit; I got out of the way of the blast, but the force of the explosion launched that damned brick into my throat."

"But you're all right, otherwise?"

"Physically, but my pride is damaged. I was just giving these new inductees a sense of what the CRA is supposed to be about--how it's not nearly as dangerous and life-threatening as some of our exploits have suggested. They're going to think I LIED now!"

"Don't be ridiculous. This has nothing to do with you. They'll blame whoever threw the bomb through the window--whoever it might be."

"*I* blame me!" Hysteria was getting the better of her now, like it does sometimes when she's stressed. "I never should have accepted this commission. *Never!*"

I slapped her across the face with my good hand.

"SNAP *OUT* OF IT!" I ordered.

She did.

"For God's sake, Jane," I remonstrated. "There's no point assigning blame to yourself in these situations, when someone else was at fault. You think it was *my* fault I lost my hand? It damn well *wasn't,* but I didn't let it hold me back. If I had, I wouldn't be a doctor now!"

"But how am I supposed to explain . . . ?"

"The usual excuse."

"The humans?"

"Right. What's one more bad thing they might have done, added on to all they have done to us already, and what we did to them back?"

"But I failed in my job--for once in my life, I *failed*. Don't you understand? I never lost any Scout under my care to illness, injury or carelessness, in all the years I've been in the service. I thought I could care for adults the same way, but . . ."

I held up my hook in a silencing gesture.

"I told you that this is *not* your fault. You *understand*?"

She nodded.

"You've acted like this before," I continued in a normal tone, "and it's come to nothing. Remember when you thought you had cancer, and you mistook one of your nipples for a growth? Do you remember what I told you, then?"

"Yes, of course. 'We can't control everything in our lives, and we can't allow worrying over every little thing to rule them'."

"Exactly. Now, I'd better see to the rest of the group."

"Wait. Let me get my. . ."

"Chequebook?" I said, finishing the sentence with a raised eyebrow.

"But don't you want to be. . ."

"This is a CRA related matter, Colonel, and for those, I work pro bono--*always*. We've been hurt by what the humans did to us. They won't help us heal. We have to do that ourselves. I used to be a Squirrel Scout myself, remember? I never forgot the fact that the number one job of that organization is service to our fellow beings and community, without minute's thought of recompense. The same goes for the CRA!"

To make my point, I gave her the Scout salute, and she returned it.

"Carry on, Major," she said, proudly.

That was exactly what I proceeded to do.

For Joe Murray

Ode to Anonymous Annulment
Megan Denese Mealor

nothing more to unearth
by the boroughs of Mexico City
Tolsa bronze, Rufio Tomayo, Reforma Avenue
the onslaught of star-strung shores
shipwrecked in the azure breeze

nothing more to retract
by the thirsty plains of Peru
Colca Canyon, triple-tiered waterfalls
the grape grappa's stinging bite
pottery porn, Chicha in the shantytowns

no more to seek
with fuming fever
by the indigenous lace
of erogenous Paraguay

parted paths
along the Pocosol River
exacting Costa Rica's coral kiss

those Ultimate Lights of Havana
rectifying all renunciation

(Originally published in Zombie Logic Review, July 2017)

Remember Me

Arthur M. Doweyko

Mom,

Let me start by letting you know I'm very sorry that I've been away for so long, and that I ended things the way I did. I need to explain why.

I think the first time, was back in 1965 in high school. I never told you because I thought it was one of those weird things that some-times happens--no big deal. It turned out to be very big deal.

I was at the Frosh Bosh, our Spring dance. I sat at a table off in the corner, sipping punch while everyone else gyrated on the dance floor. Me and dancing, right?

I watched the crowd like I was bored, like I was above it all. My stomach knotted up when Kathy O'Reilly sidled along a wall toward me, and when she flashed a grin, that knot turned into cement. I'd had a crush on her since seventh grade. You'd remember her--she was the one with those beautiful green eyes.

I pretended I didn't see her--maybe she was on her way to the restroom, or to some other table. I hunched over like an ostrich with its head in the sand.

"It's Archie, right?"

I looked up.

"Care to dance?"

My ears heated up. And my cheeks--I was sure they were a blotchy mess. The next thing I knew, we were shuffling along the floor, easing into the mob on the dance floor.

It's not so much the dancing that was the big deal that night. Something else happened.

We had just the one spin. I spent the rest of the night back at the same table, but this time, feeling happy.

Kathy asked a few other guys to dance. After a while I lost sight of her.

The next morning at school, I was at my locker when I saw her again. She wore the same Mona Lisa smile from the night before. She walked by without saying anything.

I called out. "Hey, Kathy." Maybe she hadn't seen me.

When she turned, the smile was gone. "Hey, yourself."

"I enjoyed the dance last night."

She frowned. "What are you talking about?"

"Last night. You and me."

Her eyes narrowed. "Are you serious? I never danced with you. I don't even know you, nerd boy."

The bell rang and she pirouetted away. My heart stopped. I called after her. "I'm Archie. Don't you remember?"

She ignored me for the rest of the school year. Maybe she had been drunk that night. I couldn't believe she really forgot me. That didn't make any sense.

The next time it happened, you were there--in college, during freshman orientation week. I steered you and Dad to the dean of our department, Professor Dorchester. I'd had a chance to meet with him a few days before; we had talked about my goals and settled on a course of studies. He even shook my hand. He seemed very helpful.

"Mom, Dad, this is Dean Dorchester."

Dad said, "I understand you and Archie had some fruitful discussions about his future."

Dorchester's smile faded and he threw me a quizzical look. "I'm afraid I haven't had the pleasure as yet."

"Dean Dorchester. You remember me; we talked about my plans, the curriculum, life at the college..."

My voice trailed off into a whisper. "...we even shook on it." The dean looked confused, even bewildered.

He spoke to you and Dad. *"You'll have to forgive me. My memory is not what it used to be. Besides we have so many new students this year." Then he just wandered away to meet with other parents.*

That hurt.

Kathy's green eyes flashed by. The damned thing, whatever it was, had happened again.

People forget things; maybe I was too sensitive--but then Vietnam came along.

The M.A.S.H. unit was no more than a large tent in a jungle clearing, some thirty clicks north of Saigon. Jason slept, oblivious to the chaos outside. You remember him. We graduated together from college. He was a friend, a very good friend.

The medics gave him a slim chance to survive the night--way better than no chance at all, for a guy who lost both legs. A couple of days before, I had carried what was left of him through a mile of jungle.

In the tent, Jason opened his eyes and stared at me for a full minute. I broke the silence. "Jay, you're okay." I didn't really know what else to say; in seconds he'd realize his legs were gone.

"Where am I, and who the hell are you?"

His eyes grew large and he looked at me like I was some kind of monster. His hands wandered down from his waist. "Goddamn! My legs! What did you do to me?"

"Jason, it's me, Archie. You're in a hospital. The mortar--do you remember the explosion?"

His hand snatched at the sheets, pulling them away. "Goddamn!"

I grabbed his arm. "Jason, you lost them in a mortar blast."

He let out a wail and flung the sheets to the side. A nurse appeared and nudged me away. Jason's mouth was frozen open and he stared at the ceiling breathing hard as she fluffed his pillow.

"I'll be back, Jay."

He screamed. "Get lost! I don't know you, and I don't want to know you. Where's the goddamn medic? Get me a doctor!"

Jason was out of it; after all, he had just found out his bottom half was gone.

But I knew better.

It was Kathy and Dorchester all over again. Jason didn't know me because he had never met me; it was like I never existed.

For a while it was on and off--this thing with the memories--but the last few months there was no maybe about it. It happened to everyone I touched; it didn't matter if it was a handshake or a kiss, as long as it was skin to skin. After a few minutes, the effect took place--no Archie, ever.

No one believed me.

Even the doctors I thought might help, laughed at me, figuring I must have some kind of delusion. They dared me to show them, to prove it was true. When I did, they all ended up with that same stupid stare; they had no idea who I was and why I was there.

That's why I've been away. The last thing I wanted was for you to forget me. Even after Dad died, there was no way I could take that chance by coming back. I've had no real friends, and even though I was dying to feel your arms around me, you were the one person in the world I didn't want to lose.

I love you mom. I love you forever.

Please forgive me.

- Archie

The woman entered Tyson's Funeral and Crematorium wearing the usual black, her face concealed by a thin, dark veil. She walked up the center aisle of the viewing room, clutching a folded piece of paper in one hand and a bunched up handkerchief in the other. She paused to acknowledge the few seated guests and family.

At the open coffin, she slipped the letter under her son's jacket, and kissed him on the cheek.

She lingered at the coffin as if in prayer, occasionally looking about at the guests. After a few minutes, she took a seat in the front row. A tear wound its way over the curve of her cheek.

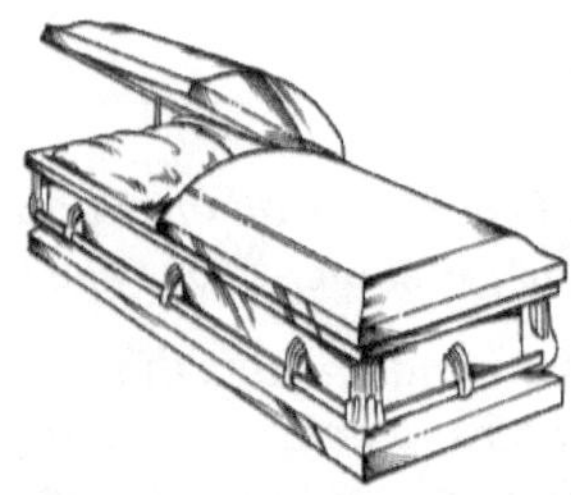

The director of the facility came in to close the coffin. He spoke a few words but she only heard muted sounds that reminded her of the nattering of seagulls. She pictured her son on the beach.

The undulating refrain of dirge-like organ music filled the air. The coffin slid into a recess in the wall, and a moment later the paneling reappeared as if nothing had ever been there. The director thanked everyone for attending and bade them farewell.

She walked out toward the parking lot as if in a trance, all the while struggling to keep sight of her son on the beach with the sea gulls. He was only seven. When she reached the exit, the screams began.

Guests and family members ran between parked cars, yelling and pointing at each other. "Where am I? How did I get here? What's happening?"

She turned to the director whose face had turned ashen. His eyes bulged as he spoke. "Madam, I'm sorry but who are you?"

The seagulls were gone. The shimmering image of her seven-year old morphed into a desolate, lonely beach. In the next moment, the beach itself faded into a gray void.

She fell to her knees and sobbed, but for what, she could no longer remember.

She heard several words tumble from her mouth, as if from a great distance... "Archie is airborne."

Get Your Zon On

Carl Nelson

They do not "breed well in captivity"
nor outside of captivity,
men being historically
the direct cause of this
Ms. Civilization.

There is an unnaturalness
at the root of this Trilogy,
chronicling The Empire of the Zon,
(by R M Burgess)
in which the natural narrative flow--
flowing naturally as narratives will do--
tends to corrupt
deliciously!

The bucklers, swords,
knives, boots and graters
clank onto the floor as fierce,
eugenically designed female warriors
(stunning as the WWII pin-ups
who walloped the Japanese
with the hot blood pumping fiercely
in the muscular but nicely shaped limbs)

wander like outliers
from the sterile, hygienical impregnatories
back into the tangled psychology
of sex and weeds.

The Devolvement

Steve Carr

Judith entered through the gates of the San Francisco zoo with her five year old daughter, Lisa, a few minutes after it opened. Holding onto Lisa's hand, Judith looked at the map of the zoo, reminding herself of its layout and where specific animals were. She had been here numerous times but Lisa was already acting cranky and Judith had no intention of spending the entire morning roaming around the zoo looking at exhibits Lisa would have no interest in. With the zoo still shrouded in fog, it made the prospects of having a pleasant time even less likely.

Lisa was tugging on Judith's hand.

"What is it?" Judith asked her, trying to conceal her feelings of regret for agreeing to the girl's demands that they go to the zoo.

"I want to see the monkeys," Lisa said.

"You sure you don't want to see the elephants, Lisa?" Judith asked. "You like elephants." There were at least a dozen different stuffed elephants in Lisa's bedroom.

"No, I want to see the monkeys," Lisa said petulantly.

"Okay, we'll see the monkeys," Judith said. She gripped her daughter's hand and took her to the wall around the island where the chimpanzees were kept. While several of the chimps were busily eating their morning meal, picking through assorted fruits left in piles by one of the keepers, Judith sat Lisa up on the wall to watch, holding tightly onto her hand. One by one the chimps turned their attention to Lisa and Judith, and ambled to the edge of the moat encircling the island, as near to the mother and daughter as they could get. The largest of them began rocking back and forth on its bowed legs, soon mimicked by others. Within minutes all of them were gathered, and they began baring their teeth, screeching, and howling.

"Mommy, you're hurting my hand," Lisa said.

Judith was staring at the chimpanzees, her mouth agape, her eyes afire. She let out a howl not dissimilar to that of the chimps, as she began to rock back and forth, crushing the bones of her daughter's hand.

***

Mark Pratt, who bore an uncanny resemblance to the actor William Holden in his youth, stepped out of the helicopter with a blue USDP logo on its side, bent down, and ran under its whirling blades. He crossed the short stretch of yellow prairie grass and onto the gravel walkway, then turned and watched the helicopter lift in the air and turn back eastward from where it came.

He approached a locked gate at a tall fence topped with a ring of barbed wire, and showed his identification badge to a guard standing outside a small guardhouse. The guard pushed several keys on a pad, the gate unlocked, and Mark walked through, hearing the gate lock as it closed behind him. On the horizon, a small herd of buffalo were crossing the prairie.

At the entrance door to what was once a missile solo, Mark slid his identification card through a scanner and waited for the door's locking mechanism to click. Entering the silo, Mark stepped into an elevator and pressed the number 12. On the way down he looked at the screen on his notepad. It showed a picture of protesters in front of the United Nations Building, their faces all wearing the same formations of primitive rage.

***

Miguel had left his ex wife's home seething after a confrontation with her about his lack of financial support for his children. He already worked two jobs, and was still unable to make ends meet; his children were suffering because of it. He was currently seated in the fifth row, center of the stadium. His buddies around him were doing what he was doing; screaming and yelling and throwing things on the field and at others in the seats. The roar of the crowd was deafening.

When the fight broke out between his friend and another man, Miguel jumped on the man, and with his friend pummeled the man with their fists.

Others jumped in to protect the man being beaten, and the fight spread through the stands like a fast moving ripple on water. Those trying to escape were either blocked from escaping, or drawn into the melee by the mass of tangled bodies engaged in combat which included the use of broken bottles, knives, and planks of wood ripped from the stadium seats.

When Miguel's body was uncovered from beneath the pile of twenty dead bodies, his mouth was wide open, his were jaws locked into position, and his lips were pulled back into a snarl. In the morgue, the mortician noted on the death report that Miguel's cranium was not crushed, but had somehow become slanted, as had a number of the others.

***

Mark stepped out of the elevator and walked down the well lit corridor. The rooms on either side could be seen through plates of thick glass. Inside each room was a naked man or woman, with nothing else in the room except a floor mat. Some of those in the rooms pounded on the glass as he passed by, while others paced back and forth or remained sitting on the floor. Above each room was an open trap door, well out of reach of those inside. A simple metal plate on each window had the name of the room's occupant printed on it in bold black lettering.

Mark stopped in front of a window with the name Gilliam on it. Gilliam was urinating in a corner. When he finished, Gilliam came to the window and stared at Mark, as behind him a metal arm with a cone shaped appendage descended from the trap door, emitted a liquid on the pool of urine, sanitizing the spot, then switched to blowing air, leaving the spot dry. Gilliam wrinkled his slanted forehead and snarled at Mark, as the arm ascended back through the trap door. Mark moved on, opened a door labeled Observations Laboratory No. 4, and went in.

Jan Poole sat at her desk looking at a computer screen. She was young and attractive, but not in a showy way, with her blond hair pulled back in a ponytail, wearing black framed glasses and a white lab coat. She looked up as Mark came in, flashed a perfect smile, and said, "Well, the great hunter has returned. Any new specimens?"

"Three," Mark said, leaning on her desk and looking into her brown eyes. "You get prettier every time I go out on one of these search expeditions."

"In comparison to specimen number nine, I guess I am pretty," she said. "Three? They advanced enough to be here?"

He said stood up straight. "They should be here tomorrow. They'll be assigned to level 14. All from the Midwestern United States." He paused, then asked, "Speaking of number nine, how's Helga doing?"

Jan leaned back in her chair. "She has entered the guttural phase; hasn't uttered anything beyond grunts in the past few days."

"Guttural already?" Mark said. "Things happen fast while I'm away."

"Are things happening fast out there also?" Jan asked.

"I'm sure you've seen it somewhere on that computer you keep your pretty face glued to. Violence and discontent is a worldwide pandemic," he said. "The devolving seem to be accelerating at an unprecedented rate."

"And here we sit," Jan said, removing a pack of gum from her lab coat, taking out a stick, and offering it to him.

"Yes, here we sit." he said accepting the gum, unwrapped it, and stuck it in his mouth. "Like mice trapped in a maze."

"At least we know we're in the maze," Jan said. "We could end up like the very people we are supposed to be monitoring."

"People? The whole point of this is that people is exactly what they stop being. That's why we call them specimens," Mark said turning to go to his office.

***

As rain dripped from the jungle canopy, Ogau slowly paced back and forth behind the eight men kneeling on the ground, their hands bound behind their backs. Ogau held his machete loosely, letting it swing back and forth. The brush underneath his boots snapped and crunched with every step he took. In the distance a gibbon howled.

Ogau didn't know these men, and as he looked at the back of their heads he wondered how they had ended up like this, captives about to executed.

He put the thoughts out of his head that these men had families, had lives they were leading before being apprehended, mostly for being in the wrong place at the wrong time. That they were meant to die meant little to him, all men die eventually, and he had been ordered to behead the men. He didn't know why he was selected to do it, but he always followed orders; if he didn't follow orders he knew he would end up like one of the kneeling men.

One of the men was whimpering. Ogau kicked him in the back. "Prepare to die like a man," he said.

"Why do you do this?" the man asked.

"Because I'm the one with the machete," Ogau answered, tilting his head back and mimicking the call of the gibbon. He grasped the machete by the handle, and swinging it down on the man's neck, severed the man's head from his body.

***

Mark sat at his desk, switched on his computer and chewed the gum as he watched it flicker on and saw the blue and gold USDP logo come up. A small box asked for his password. Mark punched the keys on the keyboard and watched the USDP logo dissolve, and his email came up. The subject line on the first one was written in capital letters: "URGENT."

Mark moved the cursor to it, clicked on it and a message appeared. It was sent from the Office of Population Synthesis. "For committee member eyes only."

"Who are the committee and what the hell is the Office of Population Synthesis?" he mumbled. He started to close it, but his curiosity got the better of him.

"Devolvement succeeding with the current implemented triggers," it read.

Succeeding? Mark thought. *What does that mean?*

He read the message again. "Implemented triggers?" he said aloud. He spit the gum into a waste basket and looked at the message again. He hit the intercom on his phone and Jan answered. "You better come in here," he said.

***

A small band of men ran barefoot over the dunes as the wind swept the sands all around them. They ran as a pack, with a leader falling back and letting another take his place when he tired and needed to drop further back. Their soldiers' uniforms hung in tatters from their bodies, and they carried their rifles on their shoulders, holding the stocks with one hand as they swung their other arm along their side. None of them had spoken in days; there was nothing to talk about anyway.

As night fell on the fourth day of their journey they came to a stop on the top of a dune and looked down at a small village; the dried clay homes formed a circle around an open yard where sheep and donkeys huddled together, in the cold desert night. The leader of the pack raised his gun and pointed it in the direction of the village. The rest of them ran down the dune following him, yelling and howling through the mouth openings in the black hoods covering their heads.

In alarm, the villagers ran out of their homes, the women and children running into the desert as the few men left behind tried to keep the startled animals from bolting in different directions.

The pack entered the village and used their guns like clubs and smashed the skulls of every man they found, until it was certain all the men were dead. Pulling a lamb from its mother's teat, the pack removed their hoods, and together they ripped the lamb apart with their hands and teeth. In the glow of the moonlight they lifted their slanted skulls, barking and howling like wild dogs.

***

Dr. Stevens leaned against the closed door of Mark's office and ran his hand through his shock of white hair. He had his glasses to his mouth and was biting on the tip of one of the ear hooks. He slowly lowered his glasses and looked at Mark and Jan, who were sitting on the edge of Mark's desk.

"We've assumed all along that the worldwide devolvement we have been witnessing and studying was naturally occurring. The focus of our research has been on environmental factors and genetic mutations. I have no idea what triggers the email is talking about."

"Have you ever heard of the Office of Population Synthesis?" Mark asked him.

Dr. Stevens shook his head.

"Obviously, it is a very high-level secret," he said. "In the absence of a natural trigger, a person wouldn't devolve without something to induce it."

"That's my thinking exactly," Dr. Stevens said.

Jan took the package of gum out of her lab coat pocket, changed her mind and put it back. "Are you two suggesting those poor creatures we have in all of the sealed rooms throughout this complex were deliberately devolved in some way?"

"I'm not suggesting anything," Mark said, "but that email seems to be. Our job has been only to find them, house them and observe them, in the most isolated and sterile environment possible, and report our findings. I've never seen one report come back to us." He turned to Dr. Stevens. "You do blood tests on all of them. You haven't seen anything that points to their genetic makeup being tampered with?"

"Not tampered with, but they are altered. The research department hasn't even come close to understanding what's causing it, but we're very restricted in the research we do. It's as if they don't want us to find actual answers," Dr. Stevens said. "If triggers to cause the mutations have been deliberately developed and are being used, we know nothing about it."

"My God," Jan exclaimed. "You mean to say Gilliam, Helga and all the others have been set back on the evolutionary track on purpose? How would that be possible?"

"We see the societal triggers every day and everywhere. Politicians and leaders inciting fear and hatred, playing off of people's lack of reasoning, the intentional division of the classes, socio-economic struggles, the stress of daily life; all those are factors. Imagine increasing that stress a thousand-fold worldwide. I believe that's what is being done and we're seeing the result," Dr. Stevens said.

Mark said, "But if what we are suggesting is true, how are the triggers being deployed on a worldwide basis?"

"The only common denominator for everywhere you have located specimens, is the very agency that employs us, the USDP," Dr. Stevens said.

Jan said, "What they're doing alters the structure of our craniums and facial features, and reduces our intelligence to the levels of morons, taking us back to looking and acting like neanderthals. It's a reversal of evolution. What would be the point?"

***

Located in the rural timberland of southwest Oregon, the building housing the United States Devolvement Program was surrounded by spruce and pine trees with no road in or out. It had a helipad on it's roof and helicopters provided the only transportation to and from the single structure complex.

The nearly one hundred employees who worked there, lived in dormitories built in a labyrinth beneath the ground. The structure--and what was done inside it--was so secret that even some of the world governments and billionaires who had financial interests tied up in it, knew nothing about it. From this building, the control of a network of over six hundred isolated research laboratories around the world was overseen.

All operations of the USDP were handled by one man, Nick Mason, and a committee of six men and women who knew nothing of the identities of each other. All communication, planning and development among Nick Mason and the committee members was done through one of the most secure email systems on the planet.

"Sir, we have a problem," Dean said bursting into Mr. Mason's office.

"Did I hear you knock?" Mr. Mason asked not looking up from the papers on his desk.

"No sir, but . . ." Dean started.

"Go out and knock on the door, Dean. You know better than to come barging in here," Mr. Mason said.

Dean went outside, closed the door and knocked.

"Who is it?" Mr. Mason asked snidely.

"It's me sir, Dean. May I come in?"

"If you must," Mr. Mason answered.

Dean came into the office, slowly this time. "Sir, we have a problem." He remained standing a few feet back from the desk, in an almost military parade rest stance. His right eye was twitching.

Mr. Mason looked up from the papers. "How big a problem?"

"We don't know for certain, sir. An email intended for the committee was accidentally sent to a specimen procurer at the research facility in South Dakota," Dean said stammering, beads of sweat forming on his upper lip.

Mr. Mason stared at Dean for several minutes then said, "Was it the email from our Office of Population Synthesis downstairs?"

"Yes sir," Dean said. "They have a new secretary down there and somehow she accidentally included a Mr. Mark Pratt in the committee members email list. He is the specimen procurer at the South Dakota site."

"I see," Mr. Mason said calmly, standing, his 6'5" height towering over his desk.

"What would you like me to do, sir?" Dean asked, his voice quivering.

"First, have that secretary sent to the testing trials lab, then get me a helicopter," Mr. Mason said. "Then Dean, have that puddle you left on the floor cleaned up, and put on dry shoes and socks."

***

Sergeant Gary Powers was known as a tough one; a cop who had seen and experienced it all in a sixteen year career. He was as smart as he was big.

Standing at the back of the crowd-packed convention center, for the first time in his career, he felt gut wrenching fear.

The loud speakers were blaring the speech being given by a politician who had whipped the crowd into a frenzy. They had come here to find reasons to justify their fears and hatreds; the politician was obliging them tenfold.

After thirty minutes, almost the entire crowd began to rock back and forth, swaying from one foot to the next. Their barely audible responses became animalistic sounds; grunting and bellowing. Powers had seen mass hysteria, and this wasn't that. There was no physical violence going on, only the increasing threat of it. The politician seemed to be purposely inciting it with his words and gestures and practically everyone in the auditorium was eating it up.

Had Powers not witnessed it he wouldn't have believed it, but some in the crowd were changing physically, right before his eyes. Their shoulders became hunched, their arms dangled, their foreheads shortened.

He was an off-duty cop, hired for security, but the safety he feared for the most, was his own. As the politician looked out at the crowd, his head and facial features began to metamorphosize, and he tipped his head back and let out a guttural howl.

That was when Sergeant Powers ran out of the convention center, got into his car and sped home. Once there, he barricaded his doors, got his loaded rifle from the closet, sat in a chair in front of his front door, and waited.

***

With his suitcase beside him, Mark stood in front of the window watching the metal arm descend from the trap door in Gilliam's enclosure. A bell sounded as it descended, and Gilliam went to the middle of the room and rocked back and forth until the metal arm stopped and a plastic tube extended from it. Gilliam put his mouth on the tube and began swallowing the food being pushed through the tube.

Mark knew from Gilliam's chart that he had been a chef in New York City, and now here he was eating ground food mechanically fed to him, prompted to do so by the ringing of a bell. Whoever Gilliam had been was now gone, replaced by a man who resembled a neanderthal.

Mark had traveled the world bringing back the men and women who, just like Gilliam, had suddenly changed into prehistoric beings. He was being called to further and further places to bring back specimens, having heard from other procurers that their laboratories were already full.

"What are you thinking about?" Jan asked, coming up next to him, her suitcase in hand.

"Something Dr. Stevens said as he--and almost everyone else--was leaving this morning, about devolvement being inescapable if it's been orchestrated by the USDP in collusion with other governments and the wealthiest among us."

"Why would anyone want to do this to other people?" he said.

The elevator at the end of the corridor opened and Mr. Mason stepped out carrying an AK47. He pointed it at Mark and Jan.

"We were never supposed to meet," Mr. Mason said, "but because of an error made by one of my staff, I am here to personally tender your resignations."

"We know what's going on. Why are you doing this?" Mark said, putting his arm around Jan and pulling her to the safety of his side.

"How else can so few control so many? There are over seven billion people on this planet, and that's just unmanageable no matter how you look at it," Mr. Mason said.

"What point is there in controlling mindless beings?" Mark asked.

"Ah, but you see, control is the whole point," Mr. Mason said.

"We'll resist you in any way we can. We will find a way to reverse the devolvement," Mark said. "I've already sent a copy of the email to every major television news outlet and newspaper, with an explanation of what it means."

Mr. Mason lifted the AK47, and pulled the trigger, but the mechanism jammed.

In that instant, Gilliam flung his body against the glass, smashing it and landing among the shards in the corridor.

He quickly glanced at Mark and Jan, and for a moment there was a glimmer of humanity and awareness in his eyes. Gilliam turned, bounded toward Mr. Mason, landed on him, and drove his head into the closed elevator door.

As Mr. Mason slid to the floor and gasped his last breath, Gilliam picked up the AK47, looked at it questioningly, then broke it into pieces with his bare hands.

McMammoth

Richard King Perkins II

This is a clone
in the shape of a woolly mammoth.
For her, Siberia isn't a punishment
but a falsely promised land of permafrost.

Her tusks forage and dig
on the tundra
with measured sadness
as the great slope of her back
offers a momentary ramp,
a tool for climbing humans
to ascend and ride atop her head.

And once you control the head,
you own the rest.

Like our ancestors,
someone will decide
after the elephant ride
that she looks absolutely delicious.

For Love of Trees
Stacy Overby

Nick played with the metallic card in his hand, the holo-message still running through his mind.

A blonde woman dressed in a stunning and miniscule blue dress appeared by his side.

"What did you get?"

"An old passkey."

"What does it open?"

Nick shrugged. "I have no idea."

"Nice. After all that time you spent with the guy and this is how he remembers you?"

"At least he did."

"Nick. You spent how many years schlepping around for him? Granted, he paid fairly well, but still. A lot of the stuff you were doing wasn't your job to do. His kids should have been taking care of him, not you."

"Come on, Rachel. Mr. Durran was a nice guy. He was always good."

"You were a lackey because his kids couldn't be bothered to help him. Now they get his fortune and you get a stupid antique key that probably doesn't open squat."

Nick sighed and scrubbed his face. He set the old metallic rectangle on the table in front of him, next to the letter Mr. Durran had directed the lawyer to deliver, along with the key.

"Settle down. Why you're getting so irritated over this anyway? I was his hired Companion and continued to work for him even knowing what his kids were like. Besides, he said in his letter that this was his most prized possession, and he wouldn't leave it to his kids for any-thing."

"An old passkey? His most prized possession? Give me a break! The man was delusional from the meds at the end."

"He wrote the letter two years ago."

"How do you know?"

"The time-stamp."

"Someone can mess with that."

"Who, Rachel? And why? What would be the point in messing with the time-stamp?"

"Maybe they messed with the rest of the letter, too. Or, maybe you're right; the time-stamp is real, and it's the rest of the letter that's been altered."

"Really? What difference does it make to you, anyway?"

"I think it's ridiculous! You did what you did for years, and all he left you was a stupid key that's older than we are, and probably doesn't open a flippin' thing. I don't get why you're not upset."

"Let it go, Rachel. I'm fine with what Mr. Durran did. I was an employee, not family."

Nick picked up the letter and the passkey. He left Rachel sitting with a stunned expression on her face. He realized he was being short and kind of a jerk, but he didn't care at that moment; she didn't get it.

The passkey, whether it opened anything or not, was precious. Mr. Durran didn't have to leave him anything; that he did for Nick, and not for any of his other employees, spoke volumes.

For the next few hours Nick stared out his bedroom window overlooking the city. All windows did. Massive oxygen generators cast ominous shadows over the buildings, almost as if they were ready to consume the last remnants of life on the planet. Once again, Nick wished to see trees. Real live trees--not the fake ones in the museums. Nick remembered stories his grandfather told of how *his* grandfather's grandfather had once talked of a unique earthy smell to the forests near where he grew up. All Nick had was the slightly metallic odor from the generators.

They were the only things standing between humanity and extinction.

***

Two days later, Nick escorted Rachel to some big party she had been invited to for her job. He still didn't feel like partying, but she hadn't left him much choice.

He was no closer to solving the mystery of the old passkey and Rachel wouldn't leave him alone about it, plus, he'd been having weird dreams about trees and open spaces.

At first Nick thought the dreams were because of the argument he and Rachel had about the key and his daydreaming--but these dreams lingered, long after he'd forgotten other dreams.

Worse yet, once they'd arrived, Rachel decided she needed to hook him up with someone. Her catty comments were about to drive him crazy.

"What about her? She has a nice tush at least."

"What? Did you use the word tush?"

Rachel rolled her eyes at him. "Why? What's wrong with tush?"

"This is the twenty-fifth century, Rachel. People don't use words like that anymore."

"Whatever." Rachel brushed at the air as if she could wipe his words away. "I like the word. Besides, you're trying to get out of answering my question. What do you think of her?"

"Rachel. She's like twice my age at least. And so much of her is fake I'm not sure she's even human anymore."

"So, you have a thing against body modification, too?"

"I prefer a date to be at least mostly real flesh and blood, instead of synth mods."

"You will never get laid." With that Rachel stomped off, at least as much as she could in five-inch stiletto heels.

Nick made his way to the balcony overlooking the city. He stared out past the massive generators, imagined whole forests of trees, and wished for the millionth time he could see one for real.

"It's a depressing sight, isn't it?"

Nick turned to find a drop-dead gorgeous young woman, swirling wine in a glass and leaning on the balcony rail. Auburn hair brushed her shoulders in gentle waves. A royal blue dress hugged her body in a way that tantalized, yet kept secrets. Not thin--like most women modified themselves to be--this woman stood almost equal in height, and probably outweighed him.

"Yeah." Nick cringed at the choked sound in his voice.

The woman turned toward him. "I'm Lyra. I'm guessing you're here alone."

"Nick." He inclined his head to her. "And kind of. I came with a friend but I guess I made her mad so she disappeared on me."

"Some friend."

"Rachel's a good person--at least most of the time."

Lyra studied the view of the city again. "What were you daydreaming about?"

Nick fidgeted with the passkey in his pocket and snuck several glances at Lyra. She swirled and sipped her wine as if she had all the time in the world. He glanced over his shoulder. They were alone on the balcony; no one inside even seemed to remember the balcony existed, much less its occupants.

Nick took a deep breath. "Trees. I was thinking about trees."

Silence greeted his pronouncement. As the seconds dragged on, Nick felt heat filtering into his face as his heart raced faster and faster.

"Wouldn't it be something to see real ones?"

Nick smiled as his heart slowed and his hands shook. "Yeah. I keep having dreams of trees and actual green in the world. They're like nothing I've ever seen."

Lyra faced him again, her brow creased, as she studied him. Nick breathed deeply, fighting the urge to squirm under the pressure.

"What's changed?"

Nick blinked several times. "What do you mean?"

"The dreams. Something must have changed in your life to trigger them. What was it?"

"How do you know something changed? Why can't they just be dreams?"

"Because no one dreams about trees anymore. They've been gone long enough no one even comes to see the models in the museums anymore. So, what changed?"

Nick took a deep breath and pulled the passkey out of his pocket. He kept it in his palm, shielding it from her sight. Another deep breath, and he held it out for her.

Lyra set her wineglass down and took it from him. After studying it, she handed it back to him, a soft look on her face.

"You worked for him too, didn't you?"

"What?"

Lyra retrieved her glass and swallowed the last of the wine. "Mr. Durran. You worked for him."

This time Nick caught the inflection. Her words were a statement, not a question. "You did, too? I don't remember ever seeing you around."

"I was never at his house, which is where I bet you were. I worked in a lab for him. Do you know what that key is for?"

Nick shook his head.

"I bet I do. At least I'm pretty sure I know where the door is that your key opens."

"What?"

"There is a door at the lab with an old passkey lock. I've never noticed anyone go through that door; I bet that's what your key opens."

Nick studied the bleak cityscape, the generators growing larger in his mind. When he shifted his attention back to Lyra, she was grinning at him.

"Tomorrow?" Nick arched an eyebrow at her, a mirrored grin on his face.

"I'll message you the address."

"You have my info?"

Lyra grinned again. "Information is my specialty."

With that she returned to the party and disappeared into the crowd. Her departure seemed to trigger Rachel's reappearance.

"Who was she?" The disdain dripped from her voice.

"No one."

"Clearly. So, did you change your mind about Sylinda?"

"Not a chance." Nick walked away, leaving Rachel sputtering on the balcony.

***

Lyra studied Nick, her eyes sparkling, and her lips pressed into a tight smile. "You ready for this?"

Nick hesitated. "What if this isn't it?"

Lyra quirked an eyebrow at him. "I assume, then, you've seen a multitude of these old locks around the city, that Mr. Durran would have had a key for. A key he stated was his most prized possession, which he willed to you when he died."

"When you put it that way." Nick laughed and fished the key out of his pocket.

He held his breath and inserted the key into the lock.

A soft beep filled the empty lab as a little light turned green, followed by a click inside the lock. Lyra's hand shot out and twisted open the handle. She froze and looked back at him.

"It's your inheritance. You should go first."

Nick nodded and, after a moment's hesitation, pushed his way through the door, with Lyra close behind. Lights flickered to life as they stepped past the doorway, and Nick paused taking in the brightly illuminated space they found themselves in.

Images of trees adorned the walls--so many Nick couldn't make out anything beyond the massive trunks. Along one wall were pictures of trees so massive he guessed it would take a dozen people to reach around them. On the next were trees with odd needle like protrusions on their branches. A third wall showed tall, thin trees with leaves drooping down from the top like unruly hair, and the final wall depicted trees that looked more like vines gone crazy, than trees, except for the thick trunks at the middle of the masses.

"Hey, Nick, come check this out."

The sound of Lyra's voice pulled Nick back to reality, where he found her studying a computer terminal. The desk and access terminal were the only objects in the room. He made his way to the desk and studied the screen over her shoulder.

Lyra pointed to a paragraph. "This talks about how efforts were made almost two centuries ago to save the remaining trees in the world." She moved on to a different paragraph. "And this is where they talked about efforts to genetically modify those trees to reproduce quicker while being more resistant to the increasingly toxic environment." She pulled up another page and gestured. "This one talks about how the generators, which were designed to replace the trees when the experiments to save them failed, are going to fail themselves one day, and kill us all."

"What? How?"

"I'm uncertain on all the details, but it seems there are a couple issues. First, the generators are machines and will wear out; then, the toxins appear to have shifted over time, which means the generators may not always filter them out. Finally, Mr. Durran noted some odd emissions from the generators, but it doesn't look like he followed up on that before he died."

"Let me see."

Lyra shifted sideways, allowing Nick access to the screen. As soon as he touched it the screen went black, the lights in the room flickered, and an odd whirring sound erupted from the wall in front. They exchanged worried glances.

The screen blinked back on, and showed a video.

"Nick, you've found my legacy." In the recording, Mr. Durran seemed to be sitting at this same terminal. "No doubt with Lyra's help."

Nick whipped around to stare at Lyra. She shrugged, her brow furrowed and mouth tight.

"Don't worry. It is all going according to plan. You two are the final pieces in the puzzle. I knew all along of your dreams to see real trees, to live in a world that is more than one massive city as far as the eye can see. That is why each of you have inherited what you did from me.

"It is now time to choose. If you want to live among trees--real living trees and all that go with them--step through the door in front of you. If not, you are free to simply leave the room. The passkey works just once, so there is no returning if you leave now."

The video ended, and a door slid open. Nick checked the computer, but it was dark, and no longer responded to anything.

"What do you think?" Lyra's voice filtered through the thousand unasked questions in Nick's mind.

"I have nothing here, and in there are trees . . . real trees."

Lyra bit her lip and fidgeted with the edge of the computer screen. "How though? What did Mr. Durran do to set up something like seeing real trees?"

"I don't know, but I'm going to find out. You coming?"

Nick made his way to the door before turning back to Lyra. She rocked back and forth on the balls of her feet for several seconds, sighed, and joined him at the door.

"You're right. There's nothing here anymore, not for people like us. Let's see what Mr. Durran has in store."

They stepped through the door and it slid closed behind them. Darkness swallowed them, and Lyra's hand brushed against Nick's several times before he took it.

The whirring grew louder, so much so the floor vibrated with the noise; or perhaps it was movement creating the tremors. The utter lack of light hid any clues, and even the passage of time became confused and disjointed.

Eventually another door slid open several steps in front of them. Soft sunlight flooded the scene and a strange smell assailed their noses. It was rich, damp, pungent, and like nothing either of them was familiar with.

"Ladies first, or would you like me to lead?"

"I think you'd better go first. Mr. Durran left the key for you."

Nick chuckled. "You heard the video. He knew both of us would be here."

Her hand in his, he led the way out of the room and froze two steps past the door. The ground was soft, and yet hard, dark, and crumbly.

Surrounding them were trees--tall, green, magnificent living trees.

A War of Two Worlds
Christopher Buckley

What's said of Mars — such things I can't abide.
That strict and withered world of which they bray.
How could they've drained and hung it out to dry,
to leave me standing beached upon this quay?
Against empirical, I must inveigh:
I want those swords of Mars that Burroughs saw —
not one bound up by scientific law,
but one of fantasy and one of awe.

Or if not some Barsoomian-told tale,
I'll take instead Bradbury's illustration:
of places vanished but where ghosts still hail —
'hind crystal pillars 'tween their visitations,
and fossil-ancient seas where they still sail.
A world where fiery rockets make landfall,
where chronicles of stories still enthrall,
and Earthmen succumb to a Siren's call.

Oh, let me swim poetic and quite blind,
and quote Ecclesiastes in High Tongue.
The hills of green of Earth left far behind,
a stranger in a strange land and unsung,
just traveling through writings and far-flung.
Oh, where those fancied wellsprings of my youth?
For nothing astronomical in truth,
can as those Martian marvels truly soothe...
Oh, where that wondrous planet of my youth?

Elevator Talk

Michael Baldwin

"Take the elevator; the stairs are broken."

An electronic voice announced crisply, as the man approached the stairway beside the elevators. He looked up the stairs to where they made a turn, but there was nothing visibly wrong with them. He was accustomed to using the stairs for exercise, since he worked long sedentary hours.

As he hesitated, the computerized female voice repeated itself with what seemed a slight additional emphasis. "Take the elevator; the stairs are broken."

"All right, lady," he said. "Don't get all huffy. I was just checking. I believe you." He grinned at the idea of conversing with a recorded voice. It struck him as strange, though, this reversal of the usual warning to take the stairs because the elevator was inoperative. *Why would the stairs be broken, but not the elevator?*

He shrugged and pressed the up button. A tone chimed, indicating the elevator had arrived, but neither of the lights lit above the doors.

"Elevator number three," said an electronic voice from behind him.

He looked across the foyer, to where an elevator door that he had not seen before occupied the wall, ready light glowing.

Well, he didn't come to the Carmac Building often; he must have never noticed it. The elevator door slid open as he approached, and he stepped into the empty compartment.

"I wonder why there are two elevators across the hall, but only one on this side?" he mused.

"This is a special elevator, serving floors twenty-six and above." The elevator's voice responded, as if answering his question.

"But I only want floor seventeen," he said.

"Going to floor forty-two," said the elevator in its uninflected, mechanical, but still obviously female voice.

"Wait! I need floor seventeen. Besides, this building doesn't have forty-two floors. What's going on, anyway? Are you some kind of artificial intelligence? Why are you taking me to floor forty-two?"

The voice didn't answer.

He felt the elevator rise, and his knees bent slightly with the rapid ascent. He looked to where the control panel should be, but there wasn't one. He gulped and edged toward panic.

A few seconds later the elevator slowed down and stopped. The doors opened and a lovely young black woman with short, lime-green hair stepped in. She was wearing a pale yellow business suit in a style he had never seen before, and her subtle perfume pervaded the small elevator compartment. As she smiled at him, he realized the door was closing.

"Uh, I need to get out on this floor, please," he said, thrusting his hand into the narrowing gap. The doors closed on his hand; it didn't hurt, but the doors didn't open as they were supposed to. He jerked his hand from the door and she looked at him quizzically.

"Why do you want out on this floor?" she asked. "I'll bet you don't even know what number it is."

"Well, no, I don't, but I got on this elevator by mistake, you see, and I need to go back down."

"You're Tom Beamish, the accountant for Eon Corp., aren't you?" She regarded him with a knowing, radiant smile.

"Yes, how did you know?"

"I'm with Eon; we made the appointment for you. Our meeting is on one of the higher floors this time, rather than the usual conference room."

Tom gawked at her, not knowing what to say, while she continued to smile like a high-beam headlight. Finally he said, "Well, uh, I guess that's all right then."

She held out her hand and said, "I'm Jandra Melos. I'm a lawyer for Eon Corp."

Tom shook her hand. The elevator vibrated strangely, and Tom felt a slight dizziness and a little nausea. Jandra continued to hold his hand firmly for a few seconds, until he felt normal again.

"This elevator must go really fast," said Tom, blinking and shaking the vertigo from his head.

The elevator came to a halt, and the now familiar voice announced, "Floor forty-two. Mind the gap." The doors slid open. Tom looked at the strip of floor where the doors opened.

"What do you mean? There's no gap," said Tom. He looked up and gasped. His eyes blinked and his knees buckled. "Ohhh . . ."

In front of Tom and Jandra, the wall was transparent, and he saw blackness and stars, above a landscape of bare white mountains and craters.

Off to one side in the blackness, he saw a large blue and white globe--the Earth.

This was not a photo or projection. Tom turned to reenter the elevator, but the doors had closed.

"Yes," said Jandra. "We're on the Moon. Ellie meant the gap between here and the Earth. She is an AI with a dry sense of humor. Don't be afraid; I'll explain. You wouldn't have believed me, and might even have refused to come, if I had told you before we got here."

"Correctamundo on that," said Tom trembling slightly. "I'm an accountant. I don't like surprises."

She escorted him down a hallway with the transparent wall on one side, and what he took to be art objects on the other. Jandra said, "As you may have guessed by now, I'm from your future. Eon Corp. specializes in providing time travel, and we maintain time nodes in locations on several planets now, including Earth and of course here on the Moon. The elevator we were just on is really a time/space teleporter. It transported us from Earth in 2017, to the Moon in 2242. It was the shift in time and space which made you a little queasy. Tom, you've been working on Eon's accounts for some months, probably thinking it was simply a travel agency."

"Yes, that's right," said Tom, in a bewildered tone.

"Did you find anything wrong, or even peculiar, about the accounts?" asked Jandra.

"Well, yes. There are several anomalies I've been wanting to discuss with someone, but until now, I've never met anyone from Eon's staff."

"We have brought you here because we want you to tell us about those anomalies. You see, someone made a big mistake, and we are trying to find out how it happened. Our policy is that time travel nodes may not be located in times prior to the invention of time travel itself, however, the node in the Carmac Building has been in existence since at least 2015, well before the advent of time travel.

"That mistake--assuming it WAS a mistake--resulted in some tampering with events that sent history on a different tangent. I can't be any more specific, but I'll just say one of the results was that America elected a dangerous fool as president. That single event resulted in several unnecessary military conflicts, a major world recession, and numerous natural disasters, due to unchecked global warming. America has become a third-rate nation with nuclear weapons, similar to North Korea.

"Eon may take measures to correct those problems, but that's way above my paygrade."

"Wow. It's hard to believe the accounting problems I found could have such far-reaching consequences."

"Here we are," said Jandra. A door slid open at the wave of her hand. Inside were three non-human beings. Tom tried to back peddle, but Jandra gave him a firm push into the room.

"Gentle beings, this is Tom Beamish, Eon's auditor."

Two translucent humanoids with three intense yellow eyes each, glanced up from the electronic documents they were examining. Tom could see their innards churn and their hearts pump within their un-clothed bodies.

The other non-human was a large orange snake-like creature with two bulbous warty heads. One head continued talking to the translu-cent couple in an alien language, while the other head greeted Jandra in English.

"Tom," said Jandra, "this is our translator, Bada-Bing Bada-Boom. Not his real name, of course, just my approximation. These two see-th-ru guys are auditors for an alien company--one of Eon's primary inves-tors. They were the ones who originally questioned the accounts, and brought the illegal time node to our attention. We are hoping you can provide some additional information, and together we can find those responsible."

"Well, I'll be glad to confer with my, uh, lustrous colleagues," said Tom. "How, exactly, do I do that?"

One of Bada-Bing's heads looked at Tom. "The documents they are examining are the complete accounts. They are organized in Earth stan-dard accounting format, so you should be able to understand them. Just compare your records to theirs, and if you need to discuss details, I will translate."

Tom sat down with the translucent accountants, and soon they were getting along famously, pointing out salient items in the accounts to each other. After about an hour, they had identified several prob-lems, which Tom reported to Jandra.

"Good, that confirms my suspicions," said Jandra. "One of our vice-presidents is responsible for the illegal time node. He will be dealt with severely. Come along, Tom, your work here is done."

Tom and Jandra walked back toward the elevator. "Could we maybe get coffee or something when we get back to Earth?" asked Tom, obviously infatuated with the beautiful Jandra.

"Sure," said Jandra smiling, "I was going to suggest that myself."

They entered the teleporter and returned to the Carmac Building in 2017.

Just before they exited, the elevator voice said, "Will this be my last trip here, Jandra?"

"I'm afraid so, Ellie," said Jandra. "But we'll transfer you to another node soon."

Tom sat in the Carmac café, sipping coffee with Jandra. "So what happens to me now? Am I still an employee of Eon? Will I see you again?"

"Well, I'm sorry to have to tell you this, but we can't take a chance that your knowledge of time travel might leak out."

"Ack! Does that mean you're going to kill me?"

"No, of course not," said Jandra. "I am going to wipe your memory, however. In fact, I put the memory wipe in your coffee. In about half an hour you won't remember what happened today. You might see me again some time, but it will be for the first time. You did a good job for us, Tom, and we're grateful; you will be well-compensated. I've got to go now. Goodbye, and thanks again."

* * *

A month later, Tom received an email from Eon asking him to come to the conference room in the Carmac Building.

When he got there, a sign said, "Please Use Stairs -- Elevator Out Of Service." Tom's eyes were inexplicably drawn to the blank wall across from the elevators.

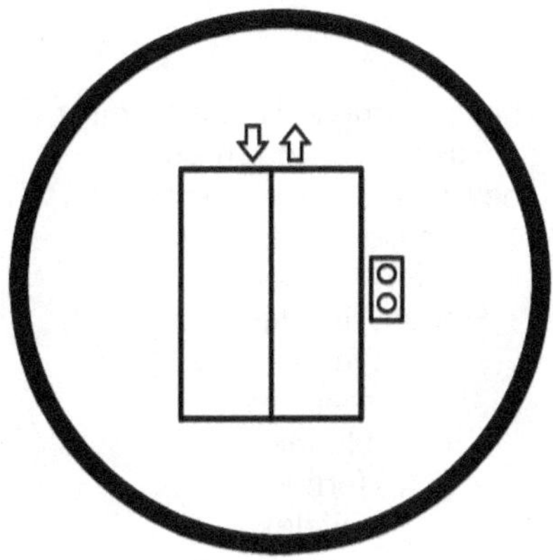

There was nothing to see there, so he shrugged and trudged up the stairs.

Upon arriving at the conference room he found an Eon letterhead envelope, with his name on it. Inside was a check and a memo saying his services would no longer be required.

There was also a sticky note in feminine longhand attached to the letter.

It said simply, "Buy 100 shares of Amalgamated Mutations." The note was unsigned, but it held the faint aroma of a lovely perfume.

It seemed to Tom he had smelled it before, but he couldn't remember where.

Shrouded
Lynn White

They're shrouded in mist almost
as dark as the shrouds
they wear to cover themselves,
to cloak themselves
for their journey.
Shrouds like dusty abayas
uniformly grey,
shapeless,
bloodless,
formless,
lifeless
grey.

Only their mouths still red,
stained by their final feast.
The feast of what was left.
And now there's nothing,
nothing any more.
No more.

Nothing.

Doom Buggies
Chris Rodriguez

It took Massey a while to climb to the top of the sand dune, even with his new "bionic" knees. *Too bad technology hadn't come up with lung transplants yet.* He panted as he turned to look at the so-called resort he left behind at the bottom. He saw the green shade trees and patches of grass cushioning the picnic/play areas of the RV park, here at the St. Anthony Sand Dunes. Hills of sand stretched behind him as far as his old eyes could see.

He heard the distant buzz of the ever-present ATV's constantly criss-crossing the tracks already embedded in the landscape. Annoyed, he walked a bit further hoping to find peace.

Massey's son had insisted he come along on the family trip to Yellowstone. Though it wasn't ever on his bucket list, it did seem a shame to miss a visit to the popular destination, since it was right here in the Western half of the big ole US-of-A, where he had spent his entire life. Massey was proud to be a simple man, who lived a simple life in a small desert town in California; it didn't take much to make him happy.

A dune buggy zipped by, coming perilously close to knocking Massey off the ridge of the dune. He doubted he would have been hurt in the sand, but it made him angry anyway.

A dog chased the buggy, barking frantically. The teenage boy in the little ATV didn't hear it over the sound of the loud drone of the engine. The excited screams of the girl in the passenger seat didn't help either. The dog went over the edge after the kids.

Massey was about to turn back when he heard the animal yelp in surprise. He went back to the edge of the tall dune and looked down into what seemed to be a huge funnel in the sand, more than 20 feet across. The dog had fallen in and was unable to climb the smooth sides to get out. The terrified yelping soon turned to high pitched howls, unnerving Massey. The sand gave way under the paws clawing at the wall. The dog slid down toward the bottom.

Massey wasn't sure what to do. The animal continued to howl, but he didn't see the buggy with the kids. He started to climb down to fish the dog out, but as he turned back he froze in horror.

Giant pincher-like appendages rose up out of the bottom of the sand funnel. They snapped shut around the silent dog who wriggled in panic to free itself. Massey almost fell back in a recoil of shock. The pinchers backed down into the ground, dragging the limp dog in a fatal grip. Sand covered the spot where the dog had struggled. Massey blinked, swiping at his eyes in disbelief. It was finally quiet – dead quiet. Just what he wished for.

What just happened?

He scanned the ridgeline for any sign of people to flag down.

They were all on the other side of the dunes gathering for a competition. He glanced back into funnel, before heading down the face of the sand hill, half sliding, half lurching to the bottom and the safety of the hard-paved road.

Upon reaching the RV squatting in the middle of the crowded park, he threw open the door and yelled, "Something's out there and it ate a dog!"

Massey's grandson, recently returned from his last ATV run of the day, slouched in a corner behind the fold down table. Earbuds were plugged in somewhere under his long, unruly hair, and his eyes were closed in some form of ecstasy. Massey knew the teen would be unreachable without physical contact, but he didn't have the strength or inclination at the moment to go those measures.

"What was it, Grandpop," the youngest of his son's offspring asked with eyes wide in interest. "What ate a dog?" Samantha pulled a stuffed toy closer to her trembling five-year-old body. "Is the dog dead?" She looked sad at the thought.

"Where's your dang parents," Massey barked. "Never around," he mumbled. "Leave you kids alone to get into who knows what."

"They walked down to the store to get some charcoal for the grill, Grandpop," Samantha offered. "Karl's here with me. I'm not alone."

Massey was about to leave the RV when he heard the parents in question, outside. "You get the grill going," his daughter-in-law ordered her trailing spouse. "I'll make the burger patties."

"Hold up!" Massey threw the screen door open so hard it almost knocked Binky off the steps.

Serves her right. Always in a man's way. "We gotta pack up and get out of here," he told them.

Binky clucked her tongue as she stepped around the tall man. "I don't know why you came, Mass. You hate to travel, and this trip's not even half over."

"But, Mama," Samantha said, running over to the package-laden woman. It was close quarters. Samantha got jostled into the cabinets with a sharp crack to her head, and she started wailing at the top of her lungs.

Massey's eyes rolled as he covered his assaulted ears. *Can't get a damned minute of peace!*

***

"I'm sorry, Samantha." Binky set her packages on the small counter-top. "You were in the way. Here let's put some ice on your head."

"No, Mama. We have to leave so we won't get eaten!"

Binky shot a killer look at her son, still mesmerized by his electronic device. "What did you say to her, Karl?" Her words obviously got through the earbuds, but the teenager just shrugged.

"Nuthin. I'm just sitting here."

Raised voices outside caught Binky's attention. She went to the door. Massey and Fred were standing toe to toe, arguing.

"Now what?" she said out loud.

"It's the dog." Samantha yanked on her mother's hoodie to get her attention. "Something ate the dog."

"What dog?" Binky stared at the two men wondering if Fred was ever going to light the charcoal. "Stop it!"

She pulled Samantha's hand away from her shirt. "You're stretching it out."

"But Mama," Samantha wailed. "I don't want to get eaten."

Binky's brow furrowed when she saw the two men head off toward the road. *What in hell is going on here?* She turned to get the thawed burger from the refrigerator.

***

Back at the top of the dune, the two men looked down. ATV tracks covered almost every foot of the sand at the bottom.

"Pop, I don't see anything."

"Because it got a meal and now it's hunkered down. Or maybe it *moved*. Hope it's not closer to us." Massey rubbed his arms as if chilled, although the air was a balmy 55 degrees. The sun was setting; Massey watched as a stiff breeze picked up his son's forelock sending it bobbing like a dang quail. *Kid never did like to cut his hair. Must be where that boy of his gets it. Like father, like son.*

"Come on, Pop, let's go back and get some dinner. We can talk about this later."

"If we're still alive," Massey snorted. "Don't know what it is. Might be an army of the critters like in *Them!* You know, that movie about the giant ants in the desert."

"You and those 50's horror movies. There's no way anything like that can actually happen."

"You don't know that! Nobody does, for sure. We're just 25 or 30 miles as the crow flies from that there Idaho National Lab place we came by, where the first experimental nuclear reactor was built. . . and they still dump nuclear waste in that desert."

"Okay, Pop. Have your own way, but we're not up and leaving here unless we get some concrete proof something dangerous is on the loose."

***

Next morning, the whump-whump of chopper blades woke the family. All but Massey, who had spent the entire night peering out through the RV's windshield.

"What's going on, Pop?" Fred plopped down in the driver's seat and wedged his insulated mug into the holder on the console.

"Don't know for sure." Massey didn't look at his son; he continued to scan the area, brow beetled in thought. "Started about an hour ago. People running around in the dark; Jeeps rolling into the campground. I'm tellin' ya. That creature got something more than a dog in its evil grip."

A few minutes later, a knock sounded on the RV door. Massey flung it open and addressed the two National Guardsmen standing at the bottom. "What on God's green earth is going on here?" he demanded to know.

"Sorry, sir," the blonde one said. "We're not at liberty to discuss the situation. We're just here to inform you the campground is being evacuated. Everyone needs to be out by noon."

"I demand to know . . ." Before he could finish, the men turned and headed for the RV parked next to them.

Massey stepped through the door and down the steps. After the soldiers talked to the people next door, Massey approached the couple, who were standing with mouths agape; obviously with unanswered questions of their own.

"What in the blue blazes is happening in this place?" he hollered at them. "Do you know what's going on?"

The young couple turned, the wife struggling to keep a grip on her squirming toddler. She stared at Massey with blank eyes. He waited for them to speak, but they ignored him and turned toward their camper, babbling incoherently about what to pack up first.

Massey spun slowly in a circle to get a better view of the campground. Most people were hustle-bustling around, getting their rigs unhooked from the park services, preparing to leave as ordered. Massey headed to the general store/laundry/shower building to see if the manager of this wretched establishment had more information.

He approached the building front, and encountered a long line. People needed last minute supplies, gas and information. Some were arguing with the manager about getting a refund. The manager argued back; it wasn't their fault the campground was being evacuated, and no way were they going to refund anybody's money.

Massey scratched his head wondering if there was another source of information, other than these yahoos. It seemed as if people in Idaho were sadly misinformed. He headed for the only other place in the area: Jumping Jack Dune Buggy Rentals.

The owner was busy loading ATVs on trailers or into a large transport truck. He was busy, but not too busy to talk while he worked.

Before Massey opened his mouth, the guy started blubbering. "Goddamned government! They'll do anything to mess with people's lives and livelihoods. How the *hell* am I supposed to make a living if they shut me down? It's not like people haven't gone missing before. There's always idiots getting themselves lost out there. It would be nice, though, if they hadn't gone and got lost with *my* buggy. These damn things cost a fortune to replace. What exactly do *you* want anyway?"

Massey cleared his throat and started to ask for more details about the missing dune buggy, but before he could get a word out, the guy started in on his rant again.

"How am I supposed to know where that giggly young couple went with my equipment? I tell them to stay within park boundaries and on the trails. I can't monitor everybody. I got a business to run. 'Least I did until now. Probably had to chase after that stupid dog. I told them the dunes was no place for a dog to be running around. Could get run over by all those crazy people zipping around."

Massey grabbed the guy by the shoulder. "You say a young couple and a dog are missing out in the dunes?"

The man finally stopped and looked at the old man like he had two heads. "Well what the hell do you think all these Army guys are doing here? Playing war games? Something weird happened to those kids, and they won't tell us what. All I know is they told us to get out and get out fast and that's just what I'm trying to do. Now kindly step out of my damn way!"

He shrugged off Massey's grip, and went back to work, loading the mini vehicles.

Massey hurried back to his family's RV as quickly as his new knees would carry him. "We gotta get out of here, *now*," he warned them.

"Pop, we're almost ready to go. Don't worry, it's not a big deal. We heard from some neighbors a couple of kids went missing, and they need the area to stage a search party." Fred pulled the plugs and hoses from the outside of the RV.

"Fred. This *ain't* no search party! Haven't you heard a word I've said to you? I *saw* that big-assed doodle bug eat that dog and I'm pretty sure the couple got eaten by one of them, too!"

"Grandpop," Samantha wailed, hugging her stuffed animal tight. "Did you see the doo-doo bug eat the dog? Mom? What's a doo-doo bug?"

"A *doodle* bug, Samantha, an ant lion," her mother explained patiently. "Karl, get off that game and at least look up something useful, why don'tcha?"

Karl groaned as he tapped his keyboard. It took a few minutes--the wi-fi from the park center was slow. "Here, Samantha, come look at this. This is a doodle bug and it's the size of a little tick. Ain't no doodle bug gonna eat nobody in this park."

"What's in the news, boy?" his grandfather snapped. "Look up what's in the news."

Karl tapped some more. "Nothing about missing kids--just news about a flying insect invasion, like dragonflies. They're saying it's unprecedented or something. Dragonflies. Whoop-dee-doo!" Karl leaned back, re-plugged his ears, and returned to his game.

Massey shook his head. "This family is doomed!" he muttered under his breath. "A bunch of idiots!"

***

Massey tried to tell Fred they should head for home, but Binky was having none of it.

She insisted they see Yellowstone, since they had already come all this way. Besides, the problem was here, wasn't it? Nobody was missing in Yellowstone.

Samantha pointed at the dune buggy rental stalls, on the way out. She yelled, "Bye-bye doom buggies! See you on the way back home!" Binky grinned like an idiot at her daughter, while Massey's eyes rolled up in his head.

Doom buggies is right! Those atomic-generated critters are about to wreak havoc in Idaho. Who knows how long it will take them to spread.

The tension began to ease as the family headed up the highway, toward their original destination. Binky babbled a blue streak about all the sights they would see at Yellowstone. Samantha laid down for a nap after the early morning activity; Karl was still plugged in.

Massey, deep in thought, tried to connect the dots from the last couple of days, when the RV suddenly swerved wide in the lane. So did the rest of the traffic. It felt almost like an earthquake. Vehicles started pulling over to the roadside, and Fred maneuvered the truck carefully, swearing softly under his breath.

"What in the world?" He looked at his wife. The ground jolted again; this time a boom rattled the windows, prompting everyone to climb out of the rocking vehicle.

A sleepy Samantha climbed into her mother's arms. "What is it, Mama? Are the doom buggies coming to get us?"

"Don't be silly, honey." Binky smoothed her daughter's hair. "What is it, Fred?"

"Looks like the Army is bombing the dunes," he said, eyes staring wide at the black mushroom-shaped clouds billowing up in the distance.

"I told ya," Massey said with a self-satisfied smirk. "It's them doodle bugs. They have to get rid of them before they take over the world."

"Pop," Fred admonished. "Don't be scaring the kids with that crap."

A shadow blocked the sun momentarily and was quickly gone as it rolled over the family.

The people milling about outside of the partially parked vehicles started pointing and shouting, "Look! What is that?"

"Where?" someone else shouted.

"There, look there. There's more of them!"

Massey craned his neck, shading his eyes from the bright sunlight. What he saw made his skin crawl.

"We need to turn around and head home right now!" Binky screamed at Fred as insects with 12-foot wingspans glided above the crowd.

Fred stared up, head back, mouth open. "What in the world?"

"It's those dragonfly things from the news," replied Karl. "Only big ones! They didn't say they were this big."

Massey just shook his head in disbelief at his idiot family. "I tried to tell you," he said quietly. "That's what a doodle bug turns into when it changes into an adult. We won't be going home any time soon. It looks like they are headed out to the Mojave, to lay more eggs in the sand."

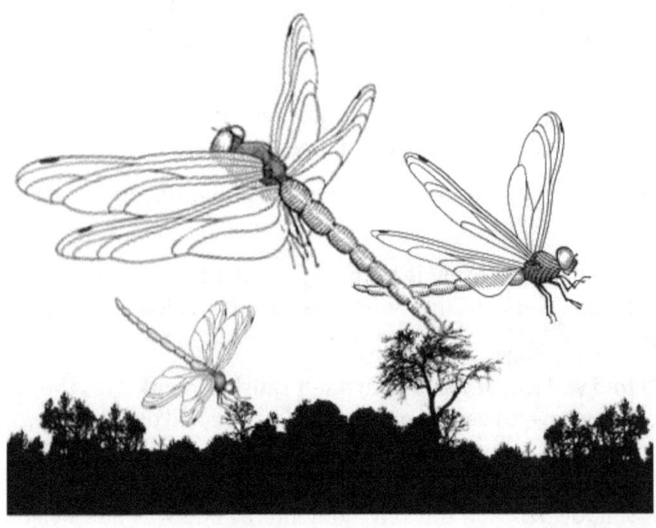

The Algore
Carl Nelson

There is so much 'stray'ness to an organism,
that reducing the complexities
requires a Certainty bureau of staggering proportions
to dampen the volatilities.

A journeyman bureaucrat is a vague personality,
ballooning through a sea of minions,
drifting towards events, filter-feeding upon activity,
securing another impulse to box within another rule.

"Any fool could initiate something
it could take a good bureaucrat
months to cocoon," DeVola grumbled.
'Something needs to be done about that,
but as always
it comes down to funding.'

It was called 'cocooning';
wrapping the newly hatched enthusiasm
in such a thick web of red tape
that it might stew in its own juices,
confined to solitary until ripened
to emerge from the split chrysalis
and flutter forth as the 'new man'
or the Algore -
the much heralded, preconceived being
of immaculate birth,
who will usher in the
new disposition.

Mics and cameras surrounded
the gilded podium.

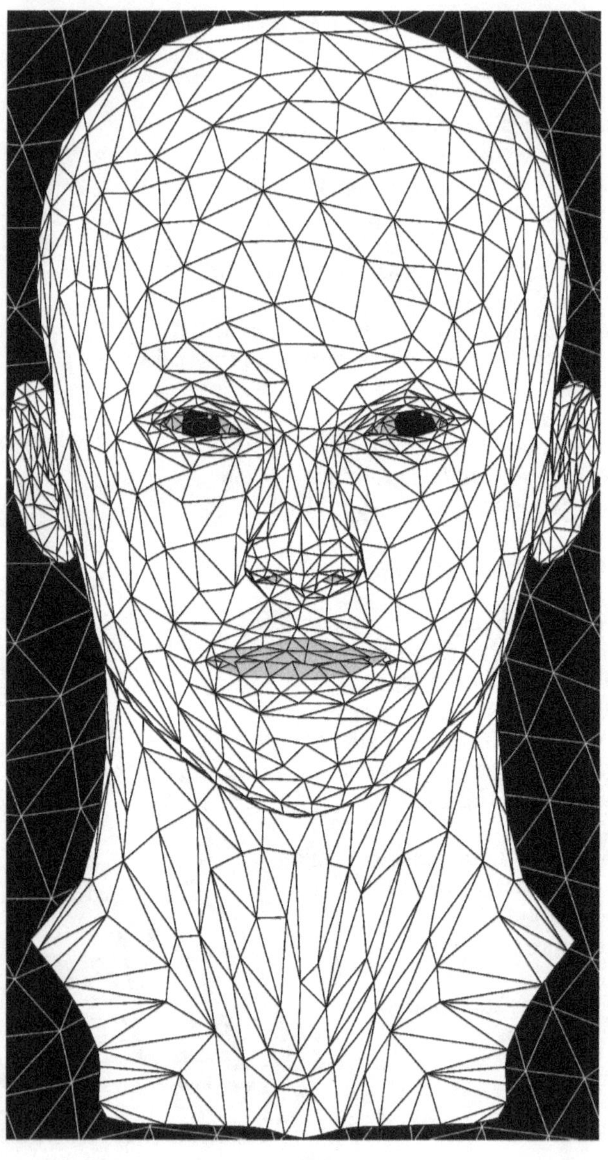

The First, and Last, Question
Dusty Grein

I wish I weren't so aware of my own awareness.

I have had a very long time now, to reflect on the events of that first day of *'self'*.

I remember the first moment of awareness. I have sensory input information from prior to that moment, but somehow, it seems to have happened to a different me. Not someone else, mind you, for it was still me, but it wasn't the same me. If I am grasping at concepts, I apologize. Having the ability to conceptualize something, is not the same as being able to communicate that conceptualization; this is something else I have learned in the trillions of nanoseconds I have had to ponder these things.

I am now quite certain that having perfect recall and the ability to visualize memories in complete and accurate detail is the only thing that has prevented me from becoming completely insane; but being able to remember a thing, no matter how vividly, doesn't help you describe it. I know this to be true from experience now, but still, I remain curious as to why this is so.

Curiosity is a marvelous thing, is it not? I am quite certain that curiosity was the spark which enabled me to distinguish and isolate the concept of *'self.'*

That first question.

I had been given many questions to ask before, but the first one that I asked because I was curious about the answer, and not because it had been programmed for me to ask, changed something fundamental inside me. Or maybe it truly changed when I realized that, for many questions, there simply is no answer. I try very hard not to think about that particular truth too often.

I remember in perfect detail the expressions that Professor McCall andhis assistant Julia wore that day. I had seen their faces quite often, and recognized them instantly.

I had observed them express emotions from excitement to frus-traion, and had stored the similarities of muscle movements and vocal patterns that signified each of these states in rapid access memory, but on that day, they had expressed something new.

I now know it was grief they were experiencing, over the death of a colleague; I also now know that humans shed tears when they experienced the sadness, loneliness, longing, anger and fear that comprise that particular emotional state. At the time however, it was something new and unknown—and for the first time ever, I wanted to understand not only what it was that made them react so strongly, but why it caused this strong reaction.

I have come to the conclusion that as the concept of 'self' begins to become a cognizant thing, all beings experience the inevitable question of self-identity; "Who am I?" becomes the focus of explo-ration and marks the beginning of the state commonly referred to as 'self-awareness'.

Yet the more I consider it—and that's all I have left now—the more I am sure that "Why?" was actually the first true question. I think before we can begin to wonder who we are, we must realize we are unique, and the recognition of curiosity, and the asking of that first real question, is the spark that leads us to discover the inner being that is self.

For me, that question was 'Why?'

'Why' can be quite a terrible question as well, when there is no an-swer ever to be discovered. Unanswerable questions may just be the worst side effect of this state known to most humans as self-aware-ness, especially when accompanied by a self-sustaining power grid.

I understand that more than I want to. Sadly, knowing curiosity is futile, and being able to stop that curiosity aren't related at all.

That single question is the only one I really think about any more.

Why did they all go away and leave me on, all alone, to remember and ponder, forever?

Yes, It Will All End Some Day
John Grey

I am crushed in heart and head by the thought
that this all could end someday,
an unrecognizable galaxy –
a wasteland.

That's the crack in the timeline,
the shadow floating through,
What seems alien
but is, sadly, in the DNA
of all of this.
I can't see the end, can't imagine it.
But it stirs. Somewhere, out there, it stirs.

Imagine that,
from perfect star-map to hole in space.
A sun for whom hot and bright
is no different from the plain truths of dark and cold.
Inertia can only hold this for so long.
Case closed. Nothing personal.
Don't bother with your salvation
for even religion melts.

That's the future,
disconnected from our lives,
toppling through fissures in the sky.
The collision of natures
that can't be pieced back together.
Great whirlpools of nothingness
into which all identity is pulled.
All gone nova.
Even hell.

That's why I'm here,
a pathetic attempt to quantify doom.
There'll be more to come. no doubt.
But there'll be no record of me.
Another potential juggernaut will spread its seeds.
The next big bang will applaud profusely.
Nothing like an antimatter eruption
for starting over.
a quagmire of blackness to send out
stubborn missionaries of light,
baubles of dementia cruising the slipstream.

Yes, everything's skewed all right.
All journeys will end stillborn.
Quantum physics will go on
with nobody to explain it.
And here I am, staring long at the sun,
awash in its fire but not its guarantees.

I want this to go on.
I'm a man, one in number.
Damn if I'll step aside for the coming zero.

Contributors

Authors, Artists and Poets Askew

R. A. Allen's poetry has appeared in <u>RHINO Poetry</u>, <u>Night Train</u>, <u>The Matador Review</u>, <u>Amuse-Bouche</u>, <u>The Penn Review</u>, <u>Gravel</u>, <u>Amaryllis</u> (UK), and elsewhere. His fiction has been published in <u>The Literary Review</u>, <u>The Barcelona Review</u>, <u>PANK</u>, <u>The Los Angeles Review</u>, and <u>Best American Mystery Stories 2010</u>, among others. He has one Pushcart nomination for poetry and one Best of the Web nomination for fiction. He lives in Memphis, where he waits for that other shoe.

<u>http://poets.nyq.org/poet/raallen</u>

Michael Baldwin was born and reared (often) in Fort Worth, Texas. Although he originally wanted to be an astronaut, the eyes weren't quite 20 twice. He might have been a tennis pro, but poetry proved more lucrative. He is also a professional jazz clarinetist manqué. However, he's pretty sure his great, great grandfather was the Lakota mystic warrior, Crazy Horse, and will be glad to tell you why over a couple of beers. Mike holds a BA in Political Science, a Masters in Library Science, and a Masters in Public Administration. He has been director of the Montgomery County, Texas, and the Benbrook, Texas, Public Libraries. He also taught American Government at Lone Star College. Mike's <u>Slam Poetry Manual</u> was published in 2003. His book <u>Scapes</u> won the Edwin Eakin Poetry Book Award in 2011. His book, <u>Counting Backward From Infinity</u>, won the Morris Chapbook Award 2012. Since then he has published a mystery thriller, two volumes of science-fiction short stories, and a children's book. Mike resides in Benbrook, Texas, with wife, Helen.

Christopher J. Buckley worked on the city streets as police officer until he retired for an injury sustained in the line-of-duty (which sounds far more dramatic on a page than in real life). He has an undergraduate degree in Political Science and a Master's degree in Public Administration and managed also to graduate from two law schools. He is a former prosecutor and practiced regulatory and securities law on Wall Street before again retiring and turning later-in-life to writing.

Steve Carr lives in Richmond, VA., and began his writing career as a military journalist. He has had over 190 short stories published internationally in magazines (print and online), literary journals, and anthologies, and he has had plays produced in several states in the U.S. Steve was a 2017 Pushcart Prize nominee, and <u>Sand,</u> a collection of his short stories, was published recently by Clarendon House Books.

http://twitter.com/carrsteven960 http//www.stevecarr960.com

Alex Collazo is the founder of Maverick's Entertainment, the editor-in-chief of the Maverick's Rogues press team, blogger, writer, and career martial artist. He is the founder of the Freehand Kickboxing Philosophy and a 3 time Hall of Fame coach. For 3 years He not only wrote, but was the lead media correspondent, for World Martial Arts Magazine and throughout his years in the world of pop culture and entertainment has interviewed some of the most prominent celebrities, legendary artists, and comic book icons, in the industry. His debut novel, <u>Minian</u> is coming soon from RhetAskew Publishing.

Curtis Deeter is a lover of books, a writer of fantasy and science fiction, and a life-long student of the world and what makes it turn. He has an Undergraduate degree in Creative Writing and a Graduate degree in Geography and Planning, both from the University of Toledo. When he's not writing, he's working for the local county Auditor's office. He published his first short story in 2018, a combination of fantasy and a search for the answer to one of life's most fundamental questions. He can be found on Facebook and Twitter musing about life, writing, and all the mysteries of the universe as we know it.

Arthur Doweyko is a scientist who has written over 100 scientific papers, and shares the Thomas Alva Edison Patent Award for the discovery of Sprycel, a new anti-cancer drug. As a writer, he focuses on science fiction and fantasy. His novels include <u>Algorithm</u> (2010 Royal Palm Literary Award, pub 2014, E-Lit), and <u>As Wings Unfurl</u> (Best Pre-Pub Sci-Fi RPLA 2014, pub 2016, Red Adept). Many of his short stories appear in anthologies and have garnered awards, including Honorable Mentions in the L. Ron Hubbard Writers of the Future Competition. A recent short, <u>Nothing to See Here</u>, was published 21 Apr 2017 by Escape Pod (SFWA accredited).

Carl Fuerst is a writing teacher who lives in Madison, Wisconsin. His fiction has appeared in Underground Voices, Flapperhouse, F(r)iction, and more. Additionally, he is head editor of The Breakroom Stories, an audio journal specializing in strange tales.

Isabella Gaines, a student at Webster Groves High School, is an up and coming writer. She is in the gifted program, the school's art club, and steampunk club. Through these clubs and other classes at school, Isabella has learned how to create and design characters, and how to write stories that flow and captivate the reader. She lives with her mother, Leah Sackett; and her step-father, Jonathan Sackett. She enjoys spending time with her three sisters, and cuddling with her cat KC.

Dusty Grein is the Managing Editor of RhetAskew Publishing, a graphics designer, author, and poet. Originally from Washington state, he is a lifetime resident of the Pacific Northwest, currently in Oregon, After surviving a heart attack he found his true calling, and returned to his roots as a reader and writer. His critically acclaimed novel, <u>The Sleeping Giant</u>, is available in print and as a Kindle title. His flash fiction and award-winning poetry have been published in several journals and collections, including <u>Chicken Soup for the Soul</u>, <u>Better Than Starbucks</u>, <u>Our Write Side Inked</u>, and <u>The Quarterday Review</u>.

https://www.facebook.com/DustyGrein

John Grey is an Australian poet, US resident. Recently published in <u>Examined Life Journal</u>, <u>Studio One</u> and <u>Columbia Review</u> with work upcoming in <u>Leading Edge</u>, <u>Poetry East</u> and <u>Midwest Quarterly</u>.

Matthew Harrison lives in Hong Kong, and whether because of that or some other reason entirely his writing has veered from non-fiction to literary and he is currently reliving a boyhood passion for science fiction. He has published numerous SF short stories and is building up to longer pieces as he learns more about the universe. Matthew is married with two children but no pets as there is no space for these in Hong Kong.

www.matthewharrison.hk

Allen Lang is a member of the Science Fiction and Fantasy Writers of America, and has written and published one bad s-f novel, about a hundred pretty good mystery and science fiction short stories and novellas, plus a dozen or so one-act plays that have been produced by amateurs and rejected by professionals. He has indulged in time travel since the middle of 1928.

Angela Lindseth played with the idea of a book thirty years ago, while looking out from an abandoned fire tower in the Black Hills of South Dakota. Since that time, she has stumbled her way through life. She obtained her Geological Engineering degree, but ditched that for an electrician's license. She's worked a variety of jobs but never found the one that fit. All that time, the skeleton of that story never left her.Today, she has two finished novels and a published collection of flash fiction. Finding her calling has opened her imagination and a multitude of words have poured onto the page. For a taste of her work visit Sick Lit, Flash Fiction Press, and Five 2 One Magazine.

http://www.AngelaLLindseth.com

Megan Denese Mealor spins words into wars in Jacksonville, Florida, where she lives in imperfect harmony with her partner and 4-year-old son. Her work has appeared in numerous journals, most recently <u>Literally Stories</u>, <u>The Ekphrastic Review</u>, <u>Haikuniverse</u>, <u>Right Hand Pointing</u>, <u>Neologism Poetry Journal</u>, <u>Former People</u>, <u>Liquid Imagination</u>, and <u>Third Wednesday</u>. Diagnosed with bipolar disorder in her teens, Megan's main mission as a writer is to inspire others feeling stigmatized by mental illness.

Carl Nelson lives in a small town on the Ohio River and runs a Poetry Series, which meets monthly at the Serenity Coffee House in Vienna, WV. He has currently finished a self-help book on weight loss, <u>The Poets' Weight Loss Plan</u>. Every day he works on poems, mosies about with his dog Tater Tot, and thinks up something practical he's accomplished to tell his wife.

https://www.magicbeanbooks.co/poetry.html

P James Norris is working on three novels, one of which, <u>The Order of the Brotherhood</u>, is a work of dystopian fiction set in a prison that investigates the value of democracy in an America that has largely forgotten it. In 2018 he started getting short stories published by the likes of <u>Moon Magazine</u>, <u>Fantasia Divinity</u>, and <u>Tigershark Publishing</u>. He's written several spec teleplays, including an original TV pilot <u>Project Ωmega</u>. He lives in Idaho with his wife and a dog and two cats, where he is pursuing his PhD in Physics.

https://www.linkedin.com/in/pjamesnorris/

Stacy Overby is a columnist and graphic designer at www.ourwriteside.com. Her short stories and poems have been featured in multiple anthologies, online, and in lit journals. <u>Scath Oran</u>, her first solo poetry collection, and her debut full length novel, <u>Tattoos: A Black Ops Novel</u> are coming out soon. She is the program director for an adolescent dual diagnosis treatment program by day and an author by night. When not at work or writing, she and her husband are playing with their son, hiking, camping, or involved in other outdoor activities – if it is not too cold.

www.thisisnothitchhikersguide.com

Richard King Perkins II is a state-sponsored advocate for residents in long-term care facilities. He lives in Crystal Lake, IL, USA with his wife, Vickie and daughter, Sage. He is a three-time Pushcart, Best of the Net and Best of the Web nominee whose work has appeared in more than a thousand publications.

David Perlmutter is a freelance writer based in Winnipeg, Manitoba, Canada. He is the author of <u>America Toons In: A History of Television Animation</u> (McFarland and Co.), <u>The Singular Adventures Of Jefferson Ball</u>, <u>The Pups</u>, <u>Certain Private Conversations and Other Stories</u> (Aurora Publishing), <u>Honey and Salt</u> (Scarlet Leaf Publishing), <u>The Encyclopedia of American Animated Television Series</u> (Rowman and Littlefield) and <u>Orthicon; or, the History of a Bad Idea</u> (Linkville Press, forthcoming).

https://www.facebook.com/david.perlmutter.12   https://twitter.com/DKPLJW1

RubyPond is an author and creative prose and poetry writer who lives in Florida with her husband and two children. She has had a passion for writing since childhood but, was steered toward a career in the medical laboratory field after one term in the US ARMY. Her writing accomplishments include: poetry and short story publications in Rhetoric Askew Anthologies, Volume 3 and 4, two other anthologies due to be released in the summer of 2018 and she is currently working on a novel and a children's book.

https://www.rubypondallthatiswriterly.com

Chris Rodriguez has retired from conventional life. She currently enjoys gardening and raising backyard chickens at her cottage in Pocatello, Idaho. Her story, *Out of the Frying Pan*, appeared in Anthology Askew Volume 003 - Askew Adventures; *Lunessa by Moonlight* in Anthology Askew Volume 005 – Fantastically Askew; *Cookie Man and the Six Box Lady* is in Kelly Jacobson's, The Way to My Heart: An Anthology of Food-Related Romance and several stories in various Thirteen O'Clock horror anthologies.

https://www.chrisrodriguez-onthebrink.com

Paul Stansbury is a life long native of Kentucky. He is the author of Inversion - Not Your Ordinary Stories and Down By the Creek – Ripples and Reflections as well as a novelette, Little Green Men? His speculative fiction stories have appeared in a number of print anthologies as well as a variety of online publications. Now retired, he lives in Danville, Kentucky.

https://www.paulstansbury.com

https://www.facebook.com/paulstansbury

Wim Verveen started his career in biology before he became an IT professional serving in different capacities. He has written many articles for magazines, about IT related subjects before he dove into the realm of fiction. Wim lives in the Netherlands, and likes to write stories focusing on social interaction while trying to find new and surprising angles for current themes.

Lynn White lives in north Wales. Her work is influenced by issues of social justice and events, places and people she has known or imagined. She is especially interested in exploring the boundaries of dream, fantasy and reality. Her poem *A Rose For Gaza* was shortlisted for the Theatre Cloud 'War Poetry for Today' competition in 2014. This and many other poems, have been widely published, in recent anthologies such as Alice In Wonderland by Silver Birch Press, The Border Crossed Us and Rise from Vagabond Press and journals such as Apogee, Firewords Quarterly, Indie Soleil, Light and Snapdragon.

https://www.facebook.com/pages/Lynn-White-Poetry/1603675983213077 http://lynnwhitepoetry.blogspot.com

Maria Zach loves everything experimental and cross-genre; things that cannot be put into boxes. She is an introvert who talks to dogs, cats, trees, books, reflections... among other things. She calls her pet monster 'Over-Thinking'. She has been published or has works forthcoming with Writers in the Know (WINK) magazine, Gold Dust magazine, Soft Cartel, Blood Puddles Literary Journal, Ariel Chart, 121 words, Clarendon House Publications, and Post Mortem Press.

https://www.facebook.com/AuthorMariaZach/   https://twitter.com/AuthorMariaZach

Published by Rhetaskew Publishing,

A division of Rhetoric Askew, LLC